The only item of furniture in the room was the bed. It was a huge old four-poster, its black lace drapes drawn back and tied to the thick carved corner poles which supported the canopy. The mattress was covered by a black satin sheet, but there were no other bed clothes and no pillows.

John closed the door behind us, and I turned to face him. He was tall and slender, his hair a shock of thick black curls. He was wearing blue jeans, a sleeveless green T-shirt and a pair of running shoes.

Neither of us spoke. There was no need for words. We knew exactly what we were here for and what we were going to do to each other. John put his arms around my waist, and his hands slid down to hold my buttocks as he pulled me against him. I raised my head slightly, my tongue coming out to meet his. My hands roved across his back, feeling his lean flesh, then stroking the taut muscles of his buttocks and thighs.

He ran his fingers through my hair, which is fine and wavy, long enough to hang down over the thrust of my breasts. And it's blonde, natural blonde.

My fingers eased themselves under the edge of his T-shirt and caressed the warm skin beneath, my nails digging in slightly as if to prevent him pulling away too soon. I held my left hand against his back, while my right explored the front of his torso, finding the web of hairs which covered his broad chest, then following them down, down, across his navel until the line of soft hairs vanished beneath his belt.

Bringing my left hand down as well, I unbuckled the leather belt and then undid the button which held the top of his jeans together. I slid his zip down with my left hand, while my right worked its way inside his shorts and found his cock. It was still curled up and felt small and soft in my hand, like a sleeping animal. But as my fingers closed around his balls, it began to awaken and come to life, stretching and growing.

Finally, reluctantly, I pulled my lips and tongue free from John's mouth. I wanted to see what he'd been hiding, the prize I now held in my grasp. John's arms released me from their tight grip, and his jeans tumbled to the floor. I pushed his yellow boxer shorts downwards and let go of his prick, watching it grow and grow, springing up towards the vertical. Then I knelt down in front of him to get a better view.

John's penis had seemed so small in my hand, but now its dimensions had increased amazingly. It was like John himself: long and slender . . . and hard.

Tucking my hair behind my ears, I leaned forward slightly as I took hold of his erection in one hand and guided it towards my eager mouth. My tongue darted out to lick the fullness of his proud flesh, and I could smell and taste the heady aroma of his maleness.

John simply stood there, accepting this as his due, although he pushed his hips forward, urging me to take him between my lips.

But I refused to be rushed. I licked for a moment, then pulled away. Teasingly, I squeezed his prick with my hand, just barely touching my fingernails against his sensitive skin. I wanted to let him know that it was my choice what I should give – pleasure or pain.

I rolled his cock between the palms of both hands, then

Blonde

SUZANNE DE NIMES

NEON

A NEON PAPERBACK

This paperback edition published in 2006 by Neon
The Orion Publishing Group Ltd.
Orion House, 5 Upper Saint Martin's Lane
London WC2H 9EA
All characters in this publication are fictitious and
any resemblance to real persons, living or dead,
is purely coincidental.

Copyright © 2006 Neon

All rights reserved. No part of this publication may
be reproduced, stored in a retrieval system, or
transmitted, in any form, or by any means,
electronic, mechanical, photocopying, recording or
otherwise, without the prior permission of the
copyright owner.

A CIP catalogue record for this book is available
from the British Library.

Printed and bound in Great Britain by
Mackays of Chatham.

ISBN 1-905619-05-7

stroked his balls with my fingertips. My tongue flickered out again almost touching him. Almost. John put his hands against the back of my head, trying to force me to swallow him; but in reply I pinched his testicles. Not much, not enough to hurt, but enough to remind him that what I did was up to me.

He got the idea, and instead he ran his fingers through my hair, rubbing at the back of my neck. As a reward, I let my tongue caress his shaft, circling the swollen glans once or twice. Then I opened my lips wider, raised myself higher off the ground, and drew his penis into my mouth.

Only the first inch, which I then blew almost out again; but on the next breath I took in even more of his length; on the third breath I swallowed another inch; and by the fourth gulp I'd taken as much as I could in a kneeling position. His manhood filled my mouth, almost touching the back of my throat.

My lips worked on the outside of his knob, my tongue from the inside.

I felt John's hands moving down over my shoulders and onto my back, his fingers clutching at the flimsy fabric of my blouse. I was wearing a see-through top. But not for long. I heard a tearing sound as John ripped the back of my blouse from hem to collar.

I didn't let go of him even when he tugged at the front of the garment, raising it up and allowing my breasts to swing free and naked. He grabbed my right arm, bending it back at the elbow and pulling the sleeve off; then he did the same with my left arm. The ruined blouse dropped to the ground between us. His hands reached down to cup my bare breasts, pressing the hard nipples against his palms.

He pushed off his running shoes with the soles of his feet,

and stepped out of his jeans and underwear. I pulled my head away from his knob, all wet with my saliva, and wrapped my arms around his waist to haul myself upright. All John now wore was his T-shirt, and I helped him yank it off over his head. I stepped back, gazing in admiration at his lithe naked body for the first time.

John moved towards me, but I raised my hand and held it against his chest. He could easily have brushed my arm aside had he wanted to, but instead he remained where he was. I pushed him back until his legs were touching the edge of the bed. He sat down, then shifted himself towards the centre of the mattress. He lay on the bed, putting his arms behind his neck, and he stared at me.

I tossed my hair back and ran my hands over my torso, stroking and rubbing my breasts, letting the nipples peek out from between my fingers. While my left hand continued to caress my boobs, I slid the fingers of my right behind the waistband of my short white leather skirt. All the time I was watching John, watching him and his cock – both of them waiting for me.

I began to swing my hips from side to side as my hand moved further down, easing under the elastic of my black silk panties. My index finger crept over my pubic mound, and John could see exactly what I was doing. My shoulders started to sway, my head to nod up and down, and the whole upper half of my body was in motion. It was as if I was dancing without moving my feet. I withdrew my hand and raised my arms above my head, which lifted my breasts and showed them to their best advantage.

All I have to do is look in a mirror to remind myself what a good body I have. Though my breasts aren't large, neither are they small; they're firm and shapely and I don't need to wear a bra. Whenever I do, the only reason is so that I can discard it at the appropriate moment.

I know I'm lucky to have such a great shape and physique, but I also take care of myself. I like to look good all the time, and there isn't a spare ounce of flesh around my waist or thighs.

At last my feet began to move as I danced slowly and sensuously around the foot of the bed, rubbing myself against the massive bedposts, gradually moving to the side. John reached out, trying to grab hold of me, but I nimbly skipped away and avoided his grasp.

My skirt was fastened by a row of buttons up my right hip. Without haste, one by one, I undid the buttons as I danced I started at the hem and slowly worked my way upwards, all the time displaying a greater and greater expanse of smooth ivory thigh. I'd have made a great stripper.

Eventually the skirt was held by a single button and I undid that one, letting the garment slide down but catching it before it fell too far, holding it between both hands in front of my hips, waving it from side to side, up and down, yet always keeping my skimpy silk briefs out of John's view.

I could see him becoming impatient. He wanted me now, immediately; but he also wanted to delay the moment, so that it would be all the more sweet when it arrived and I surrendered myself to him.

I used the leather skirt like a matador's cape, as a shield to cover my vulnerability. At last I twirled it around my head then flung it aside, and I became still. All I was wearing were my high-heeled white suede boots and my black panties.

Standing with my hands on my hips, I hooked my thumbs into the top of my undies, tugging first one side down a fraction of an inch, then the other. When the garment was half off, I pulled it back up again, as though I'd changed my mind, and I turned away. My back was to John, the fabric of my panties hiked up tight between my buttocks like a thong. I glanced over my shoulder, watching him, then I bent double from the waist, gazing at him upside down from between my legs.

Seductively, inch by inch, I thumbed down my briefs, twitching my hips from side to side. As I slowly stood up, I kicked the black silk aside. Then I spun around to face John, nude except for my knee-high boots.

He had seen naked girls before, but probably never one as naked as I was. His eyebrows lifted and his eyes widened as he focused on my crotch – as bare as the rest of me, because I'd shaven off every one of my pubic hairs. John's mouth opened slightly, and he unconsciously licked his lips. He'd been lying on the mattress a moment before, but now he was sitting up in readiness.

I was directly opposite him, and I raised my right foot and rested it on the edge of the bed, opening my legs to show him what I had to offer as I reached for the zip of my footwear. Removing the boot and casting it to the side, I lowered my leg – but not until I'd stroked the inside my thigh, running my fingers right up to the secret line of pink where it met my other leg. Then I repeated the process as I shed my left boot, but this time I kept my foot on the bed and stepped up onto the satin sheet, taking two paces until I was standing astride John.

He levered himself up until his face was only an inch from my flesh. I could feel his warm breath on my skin, and as I glanced down I saw his exploring tongue stretch up and try to reach my cunt. I straightened up, pulling out of reach for a second, then gently lowered myself towards his greedy mouth. I was already moist, my labia and clitoris swollen.

The touch of his tongue was like an electric shock shooting through my body, making every nerve tingle and pulse with fire. I rubbed my crotch across John's face, while his lips nuzzled the folds which hid my femininity and his tongue probed deep into its very centre.

I writhed with pleasure, moaned with delight. Very seldom do I have to fake it, and already I was building up in wave after wave which suddenly burst into the first ecstatic eruption of orgasm. Shuddering in helpless joy, I cried out as I experienced the first shattering climax.

John's mouth finally released me. I felt weak and drained as I slithered downwards against him, while he kissed my stomach, my navel, the firm pink tips of my breasts, my throat. He was guiding me onto his lap, and accurately I was impaled on his upright cock. It felt so good to have him inside me, his flesh rubbing against the lining of my twat. I was unable to move in any direction except up and down. His hands were on my breasts, expertly manipulating them, and a warm glow radiated from each of my nipples and flowed across the whole of my skin. John's hips jerked up and down slightly, driving his knob deeper within my vagina.

Then I began to ride him. I squeezed the muscles of my cunt against his prick as it slid within me, as though trying to grip his manhood by making my inner self narrower and tighter.

John released my tits and put his arms behind him, pushing himself upwards and forwards, and then I was losing my balance and tumbling over and down onto my back. Our bodies stayed locked together, his tool embedded deep inside me.

And then he was above me, and I was lying on my back. Now he was in control. He held me pinned down, gripping my hands helplessly above my head. He drew his hips back, almost pulling his cock free, and thrust deep into me, harder and further than before. Then he did it again, and again, and again.

I opened my legs wide to allow him further access, wrapping my thighs around his back. I reached down and around, taking hold of his balls in one hand, stroking his buttocks with the other.

John's eyes were clamped shut, his mouth open, his breath coming faster and faster in great ragged gasps as he gulped for air. We were both damp with sweat, our bodies sticking together, squelching with every movement as we rocked to and fro. We worked as one, thrusting in unison, pulling back simultaneously.

Still drilling into me, John slowly raised his body away from the horizontal. He let go of my wrists, his strength forcing me to unlock my ankles from around his back, and in a few seconds his torso was almost vertical. Then he pulled his prick free. I reached out, trying to catch his elusive cock, ready to take him into my mouth again, but he seized my arm and gestured with his head.

I knew what he meant, what he wanted, and I obeyed. Rolling over on my front, I raised myself on all fours. John's left hand gripped my left shoulder, and I felt his right against my buttocks as he guided his tool towards its target. His glans probed against my inner labia and then he was back inside me again, taking me from the rear, fucking me as strongly as before.

Slowly, but surely, I could sense the tide welling up from the core of my being, taking me higher and higher. I hoped

John wouldn't be through until he had guided me to the ultimate peak again. I could hear him breathing even faster now, feel his pulse racing and his heart pounding, and I knew that unless he could hold back it would soon be all over – and too soon for me.

He wasn't pushing so deeply now, or so powerfully; he was trying to restrain himself. I shifted my position slightly, ensuring that my clitoris was in better contact against his shaft. I didn't want to bring him off too fast, but neither did I want to lose what was so nearly mine. He seemed to realise what I needed, and one hand slid under me to fondle my tits while the other went to the aid of his cock, his fingertips expertly stroking my supersensitive cunt flesh.

I was breathing more quickly too, shoving my buttocks against his thighs, forgetting everything except the achievement of my desire. Another few seconds, that was all I needed. I started to cry out, gasping in sheer ecstasy, but I only had enough breath left in my lungs to sigh with complete satisfaction.

Even then I wasn't through, because the sensation in my loins built up again, only more so. And my whole body exploded in a thundering series of overwhelming climaxes. One, two, three . . . I closed my eyes, losing count of how many times I moaned in unsurpassed and unsurpassable pleasure.

What brought me to my senses was John grabbing me by the waist and trying to turn me around. I'd been so lost in my amazing multiple orgasm that I hadn't even noticed his penis being pulled out of me. I opened my eyes, attempting to bring myself back to total awareness.

John was holding his cock in one hand as I turned to face

him. We were kneeling opposite each other. I glanced into his eyes, and he nodded almost imperceptibly.

I leaned back, lying on my side, supporting myself on my left elbow. John approached me. He let go of his tool. I accepted it in my right hand, pulling him even closer. As his prick came in range, I thrust out my tongue, licking at his testicles. They had hung loose previously, but now they were together in a tight sack. I pointed the purple tip of his cock towards my face, stroking it up and down in my hand. It was damp and sticky.

Opening my mouth, I drew the swollen glans between my lips, alternately sucking and gently nibbling with my teeth. I tasted both sperm and cunt juice, a sensational mixture of the world's most powerful aphrodisiacs. Greedily, I devoured his glorious prick.

After a few seconds, I felt a change in the rhythm of the flesh sliding between my lips – a tremor which came from within, not from John's efforts to slide it even further into my mouth. I knew at once what this meant, and I pulled back my head just as the first creamy jet of spunk fountained from John's knob and splattered against the side of my face.

I took a better aim and directed his jerking cock towards my mouth, catching the second spurt on my top lip before taking the next one into my mouth. His prick pulsed time after time, shooting his warm sperm towards me. I licked hungrily at the end of his dick, making sure I didn't lose any of the vital fluid. When his eruption had ceased, my tongue lapped at the drops which hung thickly from my lips.

I rubbed my cheek where he'd first come, then sucked each fingertip in turn until every last atom of semen was in my mouth or down my throat. My eyes were closed, and I sighed contentedly. I sat up, running my hands across my breasts then down over my ribs and to my hips.

Opening my eyes, I flicked my hair back over my shoulders, twisted around and swung my legs off the edge of the bed. I looked at Mark.

"That was great, marvellous," said the director. He nodded and smiled at me. "That's fine everyone," he continued. "Thanks."

The two cameramen put down their video equipment; the lighting engineer pulled the plug and the battery of lamps was extinguished; the sound man removed his earphones and switched off his tape recorder. More sound would be added to the finished version, some dialogue being looped into the track. The tape from both cameras would be edited together, so that the final film would show all the best angles in detailed close-up.

Mark was the best director in the game, and he always worked with the best team. And that of course included me – the star of the show.

Mark was about thirty, although he looked older. His hair was thinning, but to make up for it his waistline seemed to thicken every week. I'd worked with him numerous times by now, and he'd long ago discovered that he didn't have to "direct" me. If he left me to behave instinctively, to act out my own erotic fantasies, then he'd wind up with the ideal video porn. All he had to do was make sure the cameras were pointed in the right direction and provide the set, plus an appropriate number of fellow performers, either male or female . . . or male and female.

"Good work," Mark said, moving his attention to John.

I hadn't met John until this afternoon, and I'd probably never run across him again. Certainly I'd never work with him again. I'd fucked him once, and that was enough. There were so many other cocks in the world to try. John had been competent, but nothing exceptional. He was there for only one reason: the audience wanted a few inches of meat, and John was it.

And I'd wanted a stud too, but then I usually did. I was very fortunate, I knew, because I was paid for my favourite activity.

"Thanks," John replied. Now that it was all over, he seemed embarrassed. He was sitting with his hands covering his limp penis. But he was no longer important and nobody paid him any attention. The technicians were packing away their gear, and Mark came to sit on the edge of the bed by my side.

"How are you fixed for the day after tomorrow?" he asked.

I turned towards him, my breasts swaying. As though unaware of what I was doing, I stroked my left nipple across his arm, where it was bare below his rolled-up sleeve. I was always teasing Mark like this, and he always did his best to ignore me. When we'd made our first film together, I thought it wouldn't do my career prospects any harm if I made myself available to him, but Mark didn't want to know.

"I never mix business and pleasure," he told me icily, as I tried to undo his pants zip with my teeth. I later discovered that Mark was happily married to his childhood sweetheart. They had numerous children, and he'd never screwed anyone else but her.

He made some of the best short sex films in the world, but he treated the whole thing as though he was running some other business. As if he was dealing in frozen vegetables or bulk concrete, or something like that. I'd never once noticed the telltale bulge of an erection inside his trousers, although usually the rest of the crew had hard-ons which rivalled the male stars". Frequently one of the technicians would have to act as a double, paid a bonus for the use of his erection, when the leading man had shot his load too soon or had only been able to dribble a few miserable drops of spunk from the end of his cock.

"Day after tomorrow?" I repeated. I shrugged, which set my tits jiggling. "Nothing so far as I know. What have you got planned?"

I rose and picked up my discarded silk panties, giving them a shake. Turning to face Mark, I wriggled into the garment, tugging it snugly against my crotch.

Mark kept his eyes on my face. "I've got the use of a railway carriage from a feature movie," he explained. "You play a girl who can't find her ticket when the inspector boards the train. You strip off, searching for the ticket, but still can't find it." He shrugged. "So you pay your fare in a different way. The inspector, the guard, maybe even the driver. Then we can finish on a comic note with the train jumping the rails. And you all think the train has crashed because of your explosive orgasms."

John had been listening. As the film crew carried the last of their equipment out and vanished, he spoke up. "Would there be a part in that for me?" he asked.

Mark didn't bother to look around. "Put your clothes on, kid," he told him.

John did as he was told. They were his outdoor clothes, whereas some of mine had been brought along especially for the film.

That reminded me, and I lifted my ruined blouse from the floor. I supposed that I couldn't really blame John for getting over-excited and ripping it from my body, but it hadn't been cheap.

Mark had pulled out his wallet and was counting a few banknotes onto the bed. Then he saw my shredded see-through, and he picked up half the money. He pointed to the remaining money on the mattress.

"You should be more careful with other people's things, kid," he said.

John finished dressing and collected the money. He frowned as he studied his pay, but then he stuffed it into his back pocket. He looked at me and half smiled. I was expecting him to come out with one of the usual remarks: to say he'd have fucked me for free, or maybe even to ask me what I was doing that evening. But when I kept my face expressionless, he simply turned and walked towards the door.

"Well," he said, "goodbye . . ."

Neither of us replied, and he went out.

"Here's your expenses," Mark told me, offering the notes he'd deducted from John's stud fee.

I took them, picked up my boots and skirt, and made my way towards the door. I'd left my other clothes in the next room along the hall. We were shooting in a house Mark had borrowed from a friend, which was where most of his locations seemed to come from.

"How much for next time?" I asked him, as he followed me out.

"Same as this," he said. "Not bad for a few minutes' work."

In the other room I pulled my tight fluffy turquoise sweater over my head before squeezing into my even tighter jeans, tucking them inside the white suede boots.

"I think it's time for a pay rise," I said. "I'm worth it, we both know that."

Mark nodded reluctantly. "I'll see what I can arrange."

"Thanks, Mark," I said, and he allowed me a swift kiss on the side of his face.

"Here you are." He gave me an envelope.

I pretended to weigh it in my hand, then opened my quilted bag and dropped it inside next to the leather skirt. I didn't have to count it, the right amount was always there. Mark was an honest trader; he cheated neither his suppliers nor his customers.

I snapped the brass clasp shut, thinking about the money. As Mark had said, it wasn't bad for a few minutes' work. But I was a professional, I couldn't be expected to do it for free. That was for idiots and amateurs. I expected the proper rate for the job, and no one had ever tricked me and got away with it.

It had all started when I was five years old. His name was Tommy, and he must have been three or four years older than me. He offered me a handful of pennies if I'd lift my dress and pull down my drawers. It seemed like a good offer, and so I did what he requested. I don't know what he expected, but he was very disappointed.

Even after so many years, I can still recall his words of complaint: "There's nothing there. I'm not paying you for nothing."

Or at least that was his intention. But I grabbed hold of his hand and sank my teeth deep into his thumb, making him scream in pain. And I didn't let go until he'd filled my other hand with the promised coins.

TWO

I used to hate men, or rather boys. My first love was horses – and my second was Carole.

Boys were rough and rude and smelly, only interested in fighting and football and pulling my hair at school. That was in junior school. Later on, I went to an all-girls school, and as far as I was concerned boys were still rough and rude and smelly, only interested in fighting and football.

I was an only child, a lonely child, and I had no real friends until I met Carole. I got to know her through the riding school where we both went. She was a year older than me, and over time we became close friends. Very close friends.

Most girls of our age were already involved with boys, but not us. We spent all our free time at the stables, mucking out and grooming the horses in exchange for free rides. We preferred to keep the opposite sex at a safe distance – as pop star pin-ups in magazines, as posters on our bedroom walls.

What we had most in common was our passion for horses. It's become a sexual cliche: the image of a girl on horseback, in her severe riding uniform of helmet, jacket, jodhpurs and leather boots, with the riding crop in one gloved hand, holding the reins in the other.

But it's a cliche because it's true: sitting high in the saddle, legs wide open with a powerful animal between them who will do your bidding with a touch of the reins or whip. The smell of the leather, of the sweating horse. And the rhythm of the beast moving beneath the rider as they trot or gallop along together . . .

It's no wonder girls have such a fondness for horses and riding. I must have experienced my first orgasm on horseback – and never realised it! Of course at that time I'd no idea what an orgasm was. I was very naive and innocent.

And I was still very naive and innocent went I left school and started at the local college. Carole was also there, in the year above me.

I often spent the night at her house, or she would come and stay at mine. When Carole's parents had to go away for a weekend, I went to keep her company. It was to be the first time we were alone together, but they knew we wouldn't be throwing any wild parties and wrecking the house. Even if we did want to hold some kind of teenage orgy, we didn't have any friends we could have invited.

My main fear was that I'd be kept awake all night, scared of the dark because of some spooky horror story Carole had told me. That had happened the previous time, when she'd been staying at my house. Carole had invented such an awful tale, of ghosts and ghouls, that she'd frightened herself too and we'd kept the light on in my room all night.

Carole was a good looking girl, tall and slim, with jet black hair which fell in natural ringlets. I remember envying her, because I always thought of myself as small and plain and plump – although when I see photographs of myself I wonder what gave me that idea. It must have been a lack of self-confidence, I suppose. And also I was a late developer, stretching and growing after most of my contemporaries.

In those days I hated my blonde hair, because it made me so distinctive. I always felt that everyone was looking at me. But now I'm disappointed if everyone doesn't look at me . . .

We met up at the stables on Saturday morning, as we usually did. After work and a ride, I went back with Carole to her parents' house. They were already gone.

"We've got the rest of the day," said Carole, "so now what?"

"I don't know," I said, shrugging, and we both sat there wondering what to do.

"How about lunch?" Carole suggested.

"Okay."

By the time we'd raided the freezer and heated up something, then eaten it and done the washing up, it was still only two o'clock. It looked like it was going to be a long weekend.

We went into town during the afternoon, listening to the latest sounds in the record store, then trying on lots of clothes in all the boutiques. We didn't buy anything, of course. But by that time we were feeling hungry again, and we each had a burger and milk shake. Then we decided to go and see a film.

There was one cinema in town, but it had three screens. The first was showing a reissue of a kids' film, which my parents had originally taken me to ten years before; the second choice was science fiction, and if there's one thing I hate it's sci-fi; the third was a sex film.

"We can't see that," I said.

"Why not?" Carole asked.

I tried to think of a good answer. "Because we're not old enough?" I suggested.

"We are," she said, which was true.

"But we don't look old enough."

"We do," said Carole, which was also true.

"I don't fancy it."

"I know that," said Carole, "but do you fancy the film?"

"Isn't it just for dirty old men?"

Carole looked at the poster. She shook her head. "It doesn't say, 'Dirty old men only.' But it does say, 'Hilarious, bawdy, you'll laugh your pants off'."

"Doesn't sound much like a sex film," I said.

"Have you ever seen a sex film?"

"Er . . ."

"Does that mean 'no'?"

I nodded my head.

"Me neither," said Carole. "But I think we ought to, don't you?" She glanced at me, her eyes wide with daring.

"Okay," I agreed reluctantly.

So in we went.

I think it was probably the worst film I've ever seen in my life, although I can't remember what the title was or even much about the plot. Not that I think there was one.

And it was all so harmless. Nothing but a few naked bodies, most of them female, and simulated sex. The men were only briefly seen in the nude, and there was certainly no such thing as a penis in the functional position. I kept glancing at Carole, wondering if she wanted to leave, but she was totally engrossed in what was happening, staring up at the screen as she filled her mouth with popcorn. When it was at long last all over, I stood up but Carole stayed in her seat, watching all the credits.

Finally, she turned to look at me. "That wasn't much good, was it?" she said, getting to her feet. "I think we ought to ask for our money back." She shook her head in disgust.

I kept my head bowed as we walked out, because there might be someone in the audience who recognised me and would tell my parents where I'd been. It didn't occur to me that even if someone did know me, they weren't going to admit that they'd been to watch a sex movie.

Sex movie! What a joke that seems now.

We took the bus back to Carole's house, but neither of us mentioned the film during the journey. When we got back, we went up to her bedroom to play some music. I was sorting through the CD collection, and Carole had disappeared. When she returned, she was carrying a tray with two glasses.

"Thanks," I said, accepting one of them and staring at the contents. It was colourless, with an ice cube floating at the top, and looked just like a glass of water. "What is it?"

"Try it," Carole told me.

I did. It was sweet and fizzy, and I drank half of it in a single gulp.

"It's vodka," Carole said.

I stared at her.

"With lots of lemonade," she added. "We can try something else later. There's whisky and gin and brandy and rum, and all sorts of liqueurs. They're my favourite."

Carole sat on the bed while I chose an album and put it on her stereo. I sat down next to her, and she nodded in approval at my choice. We talked about the music and made a promise that we'd go and see the band if they ever gave a concert in our area. Then Carole turned the conversation towards the film, although I'd been trying to forget it.

"I was very disappointed," she said.

"That you didn't laugh your pants off?"

"That was just the poster, and you can't believe advertising." She shook her head. "I thought there'd be a lot more to it than that. You know what I mean?"

I nodded, although I wasn't too certain. There'd been more than enough of everything for me.

"We hardly saw any naked men at all," she complained. "It was all girls. Bare boobs and bums. That's okay if you're a man, I suppose." Carole took a gulp of her drink, swilling the ice cube around so that it clinked against the side of the glass. "Don't they make sex films for girls to look at? Ones with lots of dicks on show." She turned to look at me. "Have you ever seen one, you know, a stiff one?"

My jaw dropped in surprise at her question, and all I could do was shake my head.

"Me neither," said Carole. "Aren't you curious? I am. I thought we might see one in the film, but no such luck. And they weren't even fucking, were they, not for real?"

I stared at her, amazed by the word she'd used. It was so unexpected, totally unlike her.

Carole was watching me, studying my reaction, and I realised that she had deliberately been trying to shock me. She'd certainly succeeded. I tried to be casual as I spoke.

"Who cares about . . . fucking?" I said, and I shuddered. "The idea gives me the creeps." Which was true. I'd never let anyone do that to me. Men were no different than boys. They were rough and rude and smelly, and none of them was ever going to even touch me.

"I know what you mean," Carole agreed. "It's hard to believe that people really do it, isn't it?" She drained her glass, still watching me. "Imagine having some boy stick his cock into your cunt."

I could hardly believe my ears. Cock? Cunt? I pulled a face, to mask my increased astonishment. "I'd prefer not to imagine it," I said, then gulped at my drink.

"I've seen horses do it," Carole continued. "And dogs. It all seems pretty disgusting, doesn't it? When we first had sex education lessons, it almost made me sick."

My reaction hadn't been quite that extreme, but I remember when I'd first been told about sex, I simply hadn't believed it. The whole thing seemed so ridiculous. Why would people ever want to do *that?*

Carole seemed to share my opinion, but she was about the only person I knew who did. Every girl in my college year seemed to have at least one boyfriend, and it had been the same at school. The other girls used to boast to each other about what they'd done or where they'd been touched, and show off their love bites – opening their blouses to reveal purple marks on the top of their breasts, or pulling up their skirts to display red passionate weals on the inside of their thighs.

And the girls at college were even more explicit about their sexual adventures . . .

"Want another drink?" Carole asked, and I nodded.

While she was gone, I picked up the CD cover and tried to imagine what the group looked like without their clothes. Men were so ugly in the nude, that grotesque lump of flesh hanging down as though it didn't belong to them. It was obscene, that was the word for it. At least girls kept their sex parts decently hidden away. Until that film I'd never seen a real man totally starkers. I'd looked at paintings and statues, of course, and I'd even seen photos of the naked men – but only out of curiosity, not because I was interested . . .

I'd preferred to look at the girls in the film rather than the men. The naked women had been so perfect, with their lovely bodies and smooth flawless flesh. The men had simply looked silly. It was easy to understand why men liked seeing pictures of nude women – and obvious why girls didn't get turned on by naked men.

Who needed men, anyway? What use were they?

Carole returned eventually with another drink. I wasn't sure what it was, and didn't ask. I simply drank it down while I ate the cheese and crackers that she'd also brought up with her.

We drank and talked and ate and laughed then drank some more.

"Have you ever had a boyfriend?" Carole wanted to know, turning the subject back to our earlier conversation.

"Not really," I said.

"Not really? What does that mean? You either have or haven't."

"Well . . . I suppose . . . I haven't."

A few boys had asked me out, but I'd always turned them down. There was something about the male of the species which I totally detested. I'd felt this way ever since I was a child, so it couldn't have had anything to do with the theory of physical sex.

"What about you?" I asked.

"Not likely! It was my brother's friends who put me off. Coming around here, all sweaty after playing football; or after they'd been to the pub, talking so loud that I couldn't help hear what they were saying. The stories they used to tell about their girlfriends. The way they laughed with their mates about what their girls did to them." She shuddered. "I prefer horses."

"Me too," I said, and we raised our glasses in an equine toast.

"And I'd much rather talk to a girl than some stupid boy. They're all so immature."

I nodded, then wished I hadn't, because the room seemed

to spin around. I couldn't understand it until I lifted my glass to my mouth and missed, spilling the cold liquid down my chin. Then I giggled uncontrollably, because I realised what was wrong: I was drunk! Not that there was anything wrong about it, quite the opposite in fact. It felt very nice.

Carole was watching me with a puzzled expression. My laughter was infectious and she also began to giggle, not knowing why, but greatly amused simply because I was.

We were sitting side by side on the bed, leaning against the wall, and we laughed and laughed, rolling about helplessly as we fed each other's hysteria. We kept bumping into one another, and I elbowed Carole lightly in the ribs while she slapped my knees. Then she put her hand on my shoulder, and I could feel the warmth of her fingers. I became silent immediately, looking at her smiling face a few inches away from mine, at her moist lips . . .

And Carole stared at me. Our eyes met. Then I turned my head away quickly.

"Shall I put another CD on?" I suggested. I didn't wait for an answer, sliding off the bed, Carole's fingers releasing me from their grip.

Carole brushed a stray hair across her forehead. "Yeah," she said, after a second. "Go ahead."

I changed the album, then returned to the bed. I sat further away this time, and neither of us spoke for a few minutes.

"Do you want another drink?" Carole asked.

"No thanks."

"Me neither."

Gradually we started talking again, this time about things like college and riding and music. Then Carole noticed me yawning, and she did the same.

"It makes you tired, doesn't it, this drinking?" she

remarked, glancing at her watch. "Maybe we ought to think about hitting the hay."

It wasn't very late, but I did feel tired. It had been a fairly busy day, riding and shopping and the movies. And there'd be no Sunday lie-in tomorrow because we had to help out at the stables then go riding again.

"That's right," I said, and I glanced over to the folding bed which stood against the far wall.

There was a spare room, Carole's brother's old room. He was older than her and had left home the previous year. But I always stayed in Carole's room, that way we could keep on talking even after we'd gone to bed.

"Do you want anything else to eat, some supper?" Carole asked.

"No thanks."

She glanced at her empty glass, then smiled. "How about a nightcap?"

"No thanks."

Carole shrugged. "Okay." She climbed off the bed, stretching. "Do you want the bathroom first?"

"No, you have it."

She nodded, reached under the pillow for her nightdress, then left the room. I collected the glasses and plates, the remains of our snack, and carried it all downstairs to the kitchen. I put what was left of the cheese and crackers back in the fridge and cupboard before washing up the handful of dishes. When I returned to the bedroom, I unfolded my bed and made it up for the night. Then I unpacked my bag, taking out my toothbrush and towel and pyjamas.

Carole was still in the bathroom. She always took ages in there. I went to stand outside, and I could hear the water running. It sounded as though she was having a shower.

Back in the bedroom, I closed the door and quickly undressed, pulling on my pyjamas. Then I sat on my bed, flicking through a magazine and waiting.

But after a few minutes, when it seemed as though Carole was going to be in there forever, I walked to the bathroom and tapped on the door.

"Will you be long?" I asked.

"No," Carole replied. "Come in if you want, it not locked."

So I went in. The room was full of steam. The door to the shower cubicle was open and Carole was standing inside.

She was naked.

THREE

I stared at Carole, unable to move, not wanting to look at her, but fascinated by the sight of her nude body, all pink and soapy.

And she looked at me, her right hand caressing the sponge to her left breast. Water dripped from the black curls of her head and those between her legs.

Carole was the first naked girl I'd ever seen. I'd seen photographs in the magazines the boys had at college, and there had been that film a few hours earlier. But apart from my own mirror image, I had never seen another nude female.

My heart had started beating faster as soon as I saw Carole, and I felt a strange stirring in my groin. My nipples had become instantly hard, pressing against the fabric of my pyjama jacket.

But I couldn't stay there, I had to leave. It wasn't right for me to be in here. Why had Carole invited me in? Why had she left the door unlocked?

She didn't seem at all concerned that I was watching her. In fact, I suddenly realised, this was exactly what she wanted!

I'd so often admired her lithe figure, but she looked even more stunning in the nude. Then I closed my eyes for a second, trying to blank out that thought. I must not see her; I had to turn and leave the bathroom.

"Wash my back for me, will you?" Carole asked. "It's hard to reach."

Not wanting to, yet at the same time unable to refuse, I stepped towards her. The shower was switched off, and

Carole turned her back to me. I gazed at the superb curves of her glistening flesh. She held out the sponge to me, and I accepted it.

As if in a dream I began to soap her back, my hand making circles on her skin, while my fingers kept touching her warm flesh.

"Ahhhhh," Carole murmured. "That's wonderful. Don't stop. That's it. Harder. Just there. Now lower down." Her muscles tensed and relaxed as I sponged her. My fingers obeyed her commands, inching down towards her slim waist and then over the flare of her hips and onto the contours of her buttocks.

Then I pulled away, dropping the sponge, trying to break free from her hypnotic body. But Carole twisted around to face me, and I stared at her breasts, her nipples, her crotch, and I became immobile once more.

She smiled at me, then reached for the tap and turned the water on. The spray gushed out, rinsing the soap from her body, splashing onto me and wetting my pyjamas.

"Why don't you take your things off?" Carole suggested.

I didn't reply, didn't move, couldn't reply, couldn't move. And I watched as Carole's wet hands reached out towards me, her fingers finding the buttons of my cotton pyjama top and unfastening them, then slipping the garment off my shoulders so that it fell to the floor.

Carole's eyes were on my breasts, and then they dropped lower. As if acting on their own, my thumbs hooked into the elastic of my pants, tugging them down over my hips, letting them drop away. I stood naked in front of her. She surveyed my body, and slowly she smiled.

"That's better, isn't it?" she said. "Now we've got nothing to hide from each other, have we?" She tilted back her head, letting the water spray onto her face and course down the valley between her ripe breasts. "Why don't you get into the shower? It's lovely." She stepped back a pace. "There's plenty of room."

Carole had been enjoying herself in the water, so why shouldn't I? It wasn't going to make any difference now what I did, because Carole had already seen me without my clothes. So I stepped over the edge, climbing in next to her, and she moved aside so that I could take the full force of the spray.

"Shall I do your back?" she asked, bending to pick up the sponge, her buttocks brushing against my legs.

I turned my back in silent acceptance. I was thoroughly soaked by now, and Carole switched off the shower and began to stroke the soapy sponge across my shoulder blades. She was right, it was a wonderful sensation. I closed my eyes as I enjoyed the unique luxury of having someone wash me.

I hardly noticed as her hands slipped beneath my arms, still softly rubbing, and worked their way towards my breasts, cupping them in her palms and gently stroking them, caressing my firm nipples between her fingers. This felt even better, and my breath came in shorter and shorter gasps.

Then her right hand slid away from my right breast, gliding down across my ribs and over my waist, brushing lightly across my pubic hairs. That was when I opened my eyes, watching as one of Carole's fingers hesitantly probed into the top of my cleft. I twisted around quickly, and her hands fell away.

We were face to face, our breasts pressed against each other's. Carole's hands went around my waist, then dropped a few inches to rest on my buttocks. I gripped her wrists, and our eyes met. I let go, then stretched towards her, my right hand reaching for her shoulder, while my left touched her hip, feeling the hardness of bone beneath the supple flesh.

Slowly Carole's face moved towards mine, as her tongue darted out to moisten her upper lip.

We kissed.

My first kiss.

Our lips lightly brushed against each other's, then pushed more forcefully until they were pressed tight together. Carole's mouth opened, and I felt her tongue lightly stroke the line between my lips. Then she pushed harder, trying to probe inside but meeting only my firmly clamped teeth. I attempted to pull back, but now one of Carole's hands was at the back of my head, holding me rigid, while her tongue kept probing.

I allowed my mouth to open slightly, and Carole's tongue eased its way inside, finding my own tongue and pushing against it. This was so unexpected that I thrust my tongue at hers, trying to force it away. But instead her tongue entwined with mine, tenderly stroking it. Carole's eyes were shut, her face turning from side to side as she rubbed her lips across mine. We were breathing the same air, and even our hearts seemed to beat in unison.

My tongue began to react, imitating Carole's actions, exploring her tongue, thrusting its way into the sweetness of her mouth, while her teeth delicately nipped at the welcome invader.

Then I came to my senses and realised what I was doing. I pulled away guiltily, but Carole's hands were still around me and I couldn't retreat far.

Dreamily, she opened her eyes and stared at me. "What's the matter?"

I shook my head uncertainly, not knowing the answer. This was all wrong. We should not have been doing this. Yet it was so pleasurable, why shouldn't we? I felt confused and bewildered.

Carole was still smiling, and gradually I also smiled. Then I laughed briefly, the laughter dissolving into a fit of giggles. Carole began to giggle, too. We held each other tight, squeezing our wet bodies together. I felt Carole's crotch against mine, and she started to gyrate her hips, pressing even harder against me. And it was just like how I sometimes rubbed myself against the leather saddle when I was riding.

I began to do the same as Carole, grinding my mound against hers, our damp pubic hairs intertwining. We kissed again, and this time there was no pulling away. Our lips met, our teeth clashing and our tongues fencing as our passion became more frenzied. Our hands were everywhere. Sliding across one another's pink wet flesh, touching breasts and nipples, hips and thighs . . .

My pulse raced, my breath coming in short gasps, and my whole body seemed to be floating in mid-air. A strange and beautiful sensation was building up within me, and I didn't know what it was because I'd never experienced it before. A kind of warmth which was growing and growing and growing. Raising me higher and higher and higher. Promising to take me to a fabulous place where I'd never been and which I could only barely imagine. And if the journey was so wonderful, then how magical would be the ultimate destination?

But before I could arrive, Carole suddenly pulled away. She was panting and gasping as she let go of me, her mouth hanging wide open. She took a step backwards, her left hand going to her right breast, her fingers squeezing the swollen nipple so hard that it must have hurt. Her right hand dropped to her crotch, the palm covering her pubic hairs, the fingertips sliding between her legs. As I watched, I noticed her index and middle finger vanish as she pushed them up inside her vagina. The fingers slid rapidly in and out. Carole sank onto her knees, her eyes still shut, her mouth wide. A low animal growl escaped from the back of her throat. Her whole body trembled and convulsed as she groaned in ecstasy.

Her writhing and whimpering gradually ceased. She opened her eyes and looked up at me.

"I had to do that," she said breathlessly, letting go of her nipple, "or I'd have burst." She removed her fingers from within herself. "What about you?"

I shrugged. I was feeling vaguely disappointed, having scaled almost to the top of the mountain but not reached the peak.

"Don't you want to bring yourself off?"

I said nothing, because I didn't understand quite what she meant. But unconsciously I was fingering my own crotch, finding it damp. Not moist from the shower, rather a kind of slick wetness. I'd only rarely touched myself there with my bare hand, but somehow it felt different now – more sensitive and more swollen, with creases and folds I'd never been aware of previously.

Carole must have realised from my expression that I didn't comprehend, because she said, "Don't you ever masturbate?"

I shook my head briefly. I'd heard of it, of course, I wasn't totally naive; but it wasn't something I'd ever tried.

Carole stood up again at last. "You ought to," she told me. "It's really great." She stared at the ceiling, as if searching for the right words. "It's really great," she repeated. "I can't explain the sensation. You've got to try it for yourself."

Quickly, I pulled my hand away from my crotch.

Carole laughed. "You aren't shy, are you?" she asked.

I began to chuckle. "Not any more," I replied, and I glanced down at myself. "What a stupid word."

"What word?"

"Masturbation," I said.

"Masturbation. To masturbate." Carole paused, then grinned and added a parody of a language lesson: "I masturbate; you masturbate; he, she or it masturbates . . ."

"And that was what you were doing just then?" I asked. "With your fingers?"

Carole nodded. "It's having sex with yourself. Who needs some boy's knob when you've got these?" She wriggled her two fingers suggestively, thrusting out her tongue from the side of her mouth and widening her eyes in an indecent leer.

I laughed at her imitation of a sex maniac, then Carole reached for the tap and turned the shower on again.

"Come on," she said. "Let's get all this soap off us." She pulled the shower head from its bracket and aimed it at me, rinsing the suds off my body. "You look really great, you know. Your breasts are so round and firm, and the nipples so pert and pretty. And it's almost as though you don't have any pubic hair at all, it's so fine it's almost transparent. I wish mine was like yours."

I turned my back, letting the water gush over my shoulders and down my buttocks and legs.

"Shall I do you?" I suggested, once Carole had finished rinsing me off.

She raised her eyebrows and pursed her lips. "I'd love you to do me," she said, smiling. But she didn't give me the shower, instead spraying herself while her other hand slid across her breasts, following the spurt of the water.

"It was in the shower that I had my first orgasm," she added. "I was douching myself like this." She was spraying her crotch now, while her free hand rubbed at her pubis. "Douching is a fancy name for shooting water up your cunt. You must have done this." She aimed the spray upwards, spreading her legs, and I saw the pinkness of her most secret place.

"Er . . . sort of," I said, and I glanced away. It was crazy after what had just occurred, but the sight of her open vagina was more embarrassing than anything else I'd seen or allowed to happen.

Carole noticed that I'd looked away. "What's wrong?"

I rubbed at my left eye. "Soap in my eye," I lied. I stepped out of the shower and went to the mirror above the basin, wiping the condensation away with my hand, pretending to examine the reflection of my eye.

"I was simply doing this, thinking how nice it was," Carole continued. "Rubbing with just my fingers because I didn't want to get any soap inside me. And the more I rubbed, the more I enjoyed it. My labia began to swell, and I found my clitoris for the first time. A tiny fleshy button which also began to swell up the more I touched it. Then suddenly – wow! My first proper orgasm. And I've never looked back since." She sighed nostalgically, her fingers and the fine jets of water continuing to work on her cunt.

I dried myself, then dusted my body with talc before putting on my pyjamas again. Carole was still amusing herself when I left the bathroom.

*

When Carole returned to the bedroom a few minutes later, all she was wearing was a towel. It was wrapped around her head like a turban. She sat down on the spare bed next to me, and without a word she took the comb from my hand and continued running it through my damp locks. It sent shivers up and down my spine, a lovely feeling.

"Is something wrong?" Carole asked, after about a minute.

"No," I answered, turning to look at her. "Such as what?"

She shrugged, her breasts swaying. "You seemed to leave the bathroom very abruptly."

"No, I didn't. I'd finished in there, that was all."

"But you didn't finish, did you? You didn't have a climax. I feel so selfish." She rested her head on my shoulder for a moment.

"Don't be. It was fine," I assured her. "I enjoyed myself, and I don't regret it at all."

"That's good," Carole nodded, her eyes sparkling with mischief. "Because we've only just begun!" She tugged the towel off her head, shaking her damp hair and spraying me with fine droplets of water. She stood up, hands on hips, and gazed at me. "Have you ever had an orgasm?"

I wasn't sure. I didn't think so. I'd certainly never experienced such an internal earthquake as had seemed to shake Carole a while ago

"Well?" Carole prompted, like a school teacher waiting for the answer to a question she'd set.

I shrugged.

"Then tonight's the night," she promised me.

I opened my mouth, but then closed it again because I wasn't certain what I wanted to say. This all seemed too organised, like a task I was being set or a lesson I was forced to learn. I'd already decided that I was going to masturbate tonight, determined to give myself an orgasm even if it took me until dawn. But I wanted to do it by myself. I didn't need Carole. She'd pointed out the route, and I could find my own way there.

Carole was standing naked in front of me, and now her hands slid from her hips towards her crotch. "Look," she said, and her fingertips pulled open her fleshy outer cunt lips.

Immediately I turned my head. This should be Carole's alone, shared with no one.

"What's wrong?" she asked, in bewilderment. "You've got to know what you're doing." But when my eyes remained focused away, she shook her head in exasperation. "Okay, take your pyjamas off. Don't be shy." She laughed, turning and going towards the dressing table in the far corner of the room.

I undid the buttons and shrugged off my jacket, then pulled down the lower half of my pyjamas. Carole came back, holding a large mirror with a round wooden handle. She passed it to me.

"Say hello to your cunt," she told me. "You've never looked before, have you? So open your legs and introduce yourself. Make friends, you'll have hours of endless fun together . . ." She turned away and left the room, letting me know that what I did was up to me.

I raised the mirror, studying my face, staring deep into my own eyes as though they were those of a stranger. Then I moved the mirror down, examining both of my breasts and their dimpled erect nipples. I still felt a kind of aching void in my loins. It was a bit like being hungry and all set to eat a meal, smelling its delicious odours and almost tasting the flavours and texture, but then discovering there was no food left.

I was sitting on the edge of the spare bed, and hesitantly I let the mirror descend even further. I opened my legs. There was too much shadow to see any detail. All I could make out were soft wisps of blonde hair and vague pink outlines. I sat further back on the bed, resting my heels on the edge and widening my knees as far as they would go, and I leaned forward to peer into the mirror, my free hand gently tracing the contours of what I could see.

After a few seconds I became aware that Carole had returned. I heard her throw something onto her bed, but I kept my attention on what I was doing, amazed at how new and strange it all was. This had been part of me all my life, but I'd been almost totally unaware of it.

"Those are the lips," said Carole, also watching. "There's the inner and outer. The inner ones, yes those, are the sensitive ones. And at the front is your pleasure button. There, yes. That's your clitoris. Give it a stroke. Lick your finger first if you want. You can bring yourself off just by rubbing your clit. Or you can stick a finger or two inside your cunt and slide them in and out. Or you can do both. Yeah, you've got it. Push in there, go on."

But I didn't. I removed both my hand and the mirror.

Carole was still staring at my open crotch, and she rubbed her hand across her pubis. She exhaled noisily between her teeth.

"You're giving me the hots again," she said, and she sat down on the bed by my side, draping her arms around my shoulders. "Give me a kiss."

Our lips touched, rubbing and nuzzling, chewing lightly at

each other, teasing the soft flesh, nibbling and sucking. After a few seconds, our mouths opened and our tongues met.

I felt one of Carole's hands on my breast, while the other slipped down my side and over my stomach; but I shut my legs firmly before her hand reached its target, and she stroked the top of my thighs instead. Her lips pulled away from mine, and she bent her head, taking my right nipple in her mouth and gently sucking, her teeth lightly raking the delicate pink flesh, her tongue caressing it to even greater dimensions. And it was marvellous.

It seemed obvious what Carole wished me to do, that she wanted my fingers to find her cunt, to explore the warm damp folds, to tease her clitoris and plunge deep inside her. But I couldn't bring myself to do that. Instead I drew back so that her lips released my nipple, and I leaned down to take one of her breasts to my own mouth.

"Ahhhhh," she sighed, as my tongue circled the nipple, my lips sucking as though it was an exquisite succulent ripe fruit, and to me it tasted even better.

Carole ran her fingers through my hair, then caressed my breasts. "Shall we go over to my bed? There's more space."

We crossed the room and sat on the other bed where we resumed kissing. After a few seconds we tumbled backwards and lay together, embracing one another.

After a minute, Carole hesitantly pulled her mouth free from mine. "I've got to do it again," she said. "I know you don't want to do it to me, but I've got to have a finger fuck." She paused. "Or maybe I can use something else. Almost anything will do. I've even used the handle of that mirror over there." As she spoke, the heel of her hand was grinding against the bony mound beneath her dark pubic hairs.

And I too could feel the tension building up within me, the pressure increasing all the time.

"You know they even make special things for women to fuck themselves?" Carole continued. "Dildoes, they're called. And there are even battery-powered ones called vibrators."

I laughed, while my right hand tentatively reached between my legs.

"It's true," Carole stated. "Don't you believe me? I'd love to try one. They come in all shapes and sizes and designs. You use them against your clit or shove them right up inside. Saves wearing out your fingers, I suppose." It was her turn to laugh. "They even have ones which shoot warm liquid up you, just like a spurting cock. But I like bananas," she added, suddenly.

I stroked my clitoris lightly, which sent a shiver of pleasure from my toes to my head. "What?" I asked, wondering what she was talking about.

Carole sat up. "Here," she said, reaching for what she'd thrown onto the bed earlier. Two bananas, green and unripe. She leaned against the wall, drawing up her knees, and for the first time I saw her cunt in detail – and I didn't look away. My finger followed the folds of my own twat as I studied hers.

"Want one?" Carole asked, splitting the bananas from each other and holding one out to me.

"Not just at the moment," I said, mystified.

She put one down and started to unpeel the other. "The shape's just right, they could have been specially designed for the purpose. You can use it with the skin on, but I prefer it peeled. Not a ripe one, because it'll dissolve and go all messy. A good firm one like this, all nice and slimy on the outside." She threw the skin onto the floor, her fingertips stroking the length of the fruit as she spoke.

She looked at me briefly. I was still lying stretched out on the bed, my head on a level with her drawn up and spread legs.

Carole reached down with her left hand, thumb and forefinger opening her labia. Then her other hand came down with the banana, leisurely pushing the rounded end against her cunt. I watched in amazement. Surely the thing was too wide. But slowly, surely, she inserted it deeper and deeper until half its length had disappeared inside her.

Her eyes were closed, and she sighed luxuriously. She twisted the banana a few degrees one way, then back in the other direction, and she groaned with pleasure. After a few turns, she started to slide the fruit a small way in and out, and I saw it rub against her labia and clitoris. She moaned even louder now.

I raised myself on one elbow and picked up the second banana, swiftly peeling off the skin. It seemed too big. I'd never get it inside me. Yet Carole had managed somehow, and she was so evidently enjoying the experience that I had to give it a try or else I'd never know what it was like. It was now or never.

I sat up opposite Carole, our knees touching. Her eyes opened at this contact, and she watched as I repeated what she'd done. I rubbed the tip of the banana against the edge of my cunt, stroking my clit. The first touch was wonderful, and I shuddered with enjoyment.

Carole reached forward, and I felt her fingers brush against my twat as she guided the fruit between my moist labia. I groaned, shutting my eyes in unbearable joy, my fingers dropping away as I let Carole take over and ease the banana into my cunt, twisting it so that it stroked the walls of my vagina, pulling it back a fraction to rub softly against my swollen clit, then shoving it even deeper.

I moved closer to her, so that we sat between each other's legs. Carole had a banana in each hand, moving them in unison so that we felt the same almost unbearable sensation simultaneously. I leaned back, taking my weight on my hands. Carole was doing all the work, but I couldn't have moved a muscle. My whole body was lost as it climbed towards the ultimate pleasure.

Then the delicious movement between my legs stopped, and I opened my eyes. Carole was holding half a banana in her hand. The one inside me had snapped. She looked at me, and we both giggled. I reached forward to pull the broken fruit out, but Carole prevented me from retrieving it, pushing me down to my previous position.

Weakly, I fell back, watching as Carole bent over me. Her head descended towards my crotch. I felt her hot breath, her warm lips and her wet tongue as her teeth seized the end of the banana. She began to eat the fruit, drawing it from me fractionally with every bite, while her tongue licked against the tender flesh of my clitoris and her lips nuzzled the warm folds of my twat.

It was the most exquisite sensation I'd ever experienced.

There was no way that I could have absorbed so much sheer delight, I had to let Carole share this.

I tried to pull away, but she put her hands around my hips to restrain me, misunderstanding my motives. I stroked the crown of her head, dropping my hands down the side of her face to her mouth, feeling her lips against my cunt, reluctantly forcing her away while I slid backwards.

Carole tugged the last of the banana free from my twat and swallowed it. I moved around on my right side, bringing my own head between her legs, reaching out to draw her towards me.

She understood, and she also lay down on her right side next to me, her head the other way so that her face was opposite my crotch while mine was by hers. I raised my left leg, bending it at the knee, and Carole did the same. She pulled the remains of her own banana free, casting it aside.

We kissed each other's cunts.

My tongue probed and caressed the soft sweetness which was at the heart of Carole's womanhood, my lips sucking at the damp flesh, while her devouring mouth was rapidly bringing me towards the absolute peak.

And as I ascended, my tongue and lips felt the first shuddering ripples within Carole's cunt as she too began to climax. Our hands and fingers clawed at one another in helpless abandon.

It was beyond all imagining. I shook and trembled, moaned and cried out, every sense more aware than ever before, and my whole being surged into ultimate ecstasy as I experienced my first explosive orgasm.

FOUR

When I woke up the next morning, I was in bed with Carole, our limbs intertwined. It was so nice simply to lie there in her arms, watching her sleeping face. I'd never felt so content in my life. At last her eyes twitched as she floated towards consciousness, and then she blinked and was awake.

"Hello," she said, smiling, as she hugged me close against her nude body.

"Hello," I echoed, kissing her lightly on the lips.

"That was a wonderful night, wasn't it?"

"What night?" I asked.

Carole frowned, puzzled. Then she laughed and tugged playfully at my pubic hairs. "For a moment I thought I'd been dreaming," she told me.

"It was great," I agreed at last. "Thanks for inviting me around. Did you have my seduction all planned out?"

She shook her head. "How could I have planned that? But I did have my hopes, although I never imagined it could have worked out so well." She smiled as she remembered.

"Have you ever done that before?" I asked.

"Done what? I've done everything a girl can do by herself, or I think I have. But with two of us, it's far more than twice as good."

"Then you haven't been to bed with another girl?"

Carole looked surprised. She shook her head. "No, of course not. You're the first. What I really wanted to discover was what it's like to have my cunt licked. That's about the only thing I can't manage on my own! And I bet a girl can perform cunnilingus better than any man."

"Cunny what?"

"Cunnilingus. It means cunt sucking."

"You're kidding," I said. "There can't be a word for that." But until a few hours ago I'd never even guessed such a thing was ever done or even possible; the idea would have repulsed me. It was such a terrific experience, however, that I could hardly wait to try it again . . .

"Of course there is," Carole assured me. "There's a word for everything. There's even a word for us."

"Us?"

"We're both lesbians now, aren't we?"

"Lesbians," I repeated, rolling the sound around my mouth. The idea of sex without men had always seemed very attractive, sort of clean and wholesome. And as Carole had implied, who knew a girl's sexual preferences better than another girl?

"How about some breakfast?" Carole asked, stretching out her arms, the bed covers falling off to expose the roundness of her breasts.

"Breakfast in bed?" I said, raising my eyebrows.

"Good idea." She nodded thoughtfully. Our eyes met. "And I know exactly what I'd like to eat . . ."

That Sunday morning, for the first time in ages, neither of us went horse riding.

After that, Carole and I remained the most intimate of friends. We went everywhere together, did everything together. We even went on holiday together, sharing the same room, the same bed – and of course each other's bodies. But as time went by, we began to drift apart. Our passion was no longer so intense, the flames dying down over time.

Then Carole found another lover. His name was Peter. I don't know whether it was worse her going off with a man rather than another girl, but it took me a long time to get over her treachery. One day we were sharing a double-headed vibrator, and the next she was sharing a double bed with this guy Peter.

By then, I was working in one of the offices of the largest company in town. There were five other girls there, all of them within a few years of my own age. The office was run by a fifty-year-old sexless tyrant. The only way of telling she was a woman was by her name, Miss Tresson.

Because I was the office junior, I was given the most boring and menial tasks to do. But I got on quite well with the other five, and a few of us would go out for lunch once a week as a change from the canteen. Sometimes we might even get together for a drink in the evening, although this was rare because the others all had boyfriends, either steadies or a whole sequence of lovers.

I was very lonely. It was easy for girls to pick up men, but to find other girls was so much more difficult. A couple of the girls from the office were always trying to fix me up with dates, because they thought I was too shy to find myself a boyfriend. There was no way that I could tell them what it was I really needed. To make it worse, I fell in love with one of the girls.

Her name was Sue, a petite redhead a year or two older than me. I loved the way she reached out to touch me or put her arm around me when she was showing me what to do at work. But she also did this to the other girls in the office. It was her friendly manner, it had no sexual implications. Except to me.

Sue had a number of boyfriends, and she'd often confide

in me about the trouble they gave her, the things she had to put up with. But she never learned. There would always be another man in her life to treat her as badly as the others. Yet she could have had me. I loved her far more than any male ever would, could do things for her that she'd never imagined possible. I'd lie awake in my lonely bed, masturbating, and wishing that Sue was there with me; then I'd dream an erotic fantasy about her, and that would leave me even more frustrated.

The next day I'd see her again, watching her mouth as she talked to me and wishing I could taste those soft red lips and that delicious pink tongue, trying not to gaze too long at the rise of her upturned breasts, wondering what she looked like in the nude, unable to ignore the image of Sue's cropped red hair between my legs as her tongue thrust deep into my aching cunt.

Twice I even went out on dates with Sue, to keep her company when she'd arranged to meet some guy and his friend. Both times I hoped that it would be she and I who paired off, but it didn't work out like that. What happened was that I'd be stuck with some ape who thought that for the price of a couple of drinks he was entitled to shove his prick into me, or at the very least stuff his tongue down my throat. Each time I managed to get away safely, but the story got back to Sue – and I couldn't forgive her for passing it on to the others in the office. She didn't mean any harm by it, I know. The rest of them treated it as a joke, thinking that I must be very innocent and scared of men. The latter might have been true, but the first certainly wasn't.

The girls had arranged to go to a nightclub called The Castle, and they invited me to join them.

"I know we've been rotten to you lately," Sue said one

lunchtime, "teasing you about those men you met. So why don't you come along? It should be a laugh. It's a girls-only night."

That was what clinched it. Girls only. I'd never been to The Castle before, although I'd heard it was meant to be quite a place.

"Okay," I agreed, thinking what a good time I'd often had when I'd been out in the evenings with them. I didn't know what was meant by a girls-only night, but it sounded promising. Maybe I could meet up with another girl who shared my own sexual preferences.

"That's good," Sue told me, "because we've already got you this." She opened her bag and handed me the ticket. It was dated for the following Friday. Then I saw the price.

"You had to pay for it?" I asked.

"That's right. It's to cover the hire of the room, pay for the entertainment and for food. Drinks come extra. You drink as much as you can pay for." Sue smiled at me, and I tried not to stare at her perfect lips.

"It sounds quite elaborate," I said, reaching for my purse and opening it. "What kind of entertainment?" I counted out the money and offered it to her.

But Sue shook her head. "No, no, no," she said. "The rest of us paid for you. We go every year, and it's a tradition that the junior doesn't have to pay, because of what she has to put up with the rest of the time."

"Are you sure?" I didn't want any special favours.

"Sure I'm sure. When I started here a couple of years ago, the others paid for me." She stared absently up at the ceiling for a moment, as though reminiscing, and she half smiled. "It's a chance for all the girls who work here to let our hair down, away from husbands and boyfriends."

"Does Miss Tresson go?" I asked, wondering if it was possible for our supervisor to let her hair down.

Sue laughed out loud and shook her head. "No," she promised, "she certainly doesn't."

So the next Friday, I put on my best clothes – a pair of tight black satin pants, a bright red cotton blouse and jet black velvet waistcoat, as well as a pair of red leather ankle boots – donned my woollen coat and went off to rendezvous with Sue.

We went in through the entrance of The Castle, showing our tickets to the doorman, and he directed us up a flight of stairs to a room on the top floor. There must have been about two hundred woman in there, sitting at the tables which lined two opposite walls, or standing by the bar which ran the full length of the wall by the entrance. There was a stage against the far wall, and a disc jockey was up there playing records. She was female, as were the staff behind the bar.

The lights were turned low, a rainbow sequence of coloured spotlights spinning from a complex array in the centre of the ceiling, flashing in rhythm to the pounding disco beat. Several girls were dancing, and I glanced at them. Sue and I found the other four from our office – Jean and Trisha, Linda and Rose – and I bought them all a drink because they'd paid for my ticket. The drinks came to more than the price of my ticket, but the money didn't matter. As soon as I'd stepped through the door, I knew I was going to enjoy myself; and after a couple of drinks I was convinced of it. Two hundred girls? I was bound to find one who shared my unusual tastes.

The other four had taken over one of the round tables on the left hand side of the room, about halfway towards the low stage, and we talked about all kinds of things. We had to raise our voices to make ourselves heard above the music, and the only taboo subject was work.

I was watching the dancers, my fingers tapping the table top, and Sue must have noticed because she said: "Shall we go and dance?"

I stared at her, trying not to show my eagerness, and I shrugged. "Could do," I said casually, rising to my feet.

We walked towards the centre of the room, and I was a couple of paces behind Sue, watching the sway of her hips. She was snapping her fingers, her shoulders rocking from side to side with the beat. Then she stopped, half turned towards me, and she started dancing. I stayed a few feet from her as my body also began to move, watching her all the time. But Sue wasn't looking at me, only through me. I knew she'd come out here in response to the music – that she simply wanted to dance, it had nothing to do with me – but I couldn't accept that on an emotional level.

I longed for a slow number to be played, so that I could hold the slim redhead in my arms and pull her close against me, letting my touch demonstrate what I felt for her; but there was little chance of that.

I stared at the way she moved, at her arms and legs flowing with the rhythm, at her breasts gently bouncing up and down, and I thought of how she would look when her body was twisting and writhing in the ecstasy of lovemaking. And I knew it was futile, that she would never be mine.

So I began to focus my attention elsewhere, searching for a pair of eyes which would meet and hold my own. I must have been quite a distinctive figure with my flowing blonde hair, my breasts jiggling unfettered beneath my blouse. But whenever I noticed another girl watching me and I turned my head, she would glance away.

After a few minutes, the music faded away, the flashing coloured lights ceased to revolve, and some of the main lighting came on again.

"If you want to take your places, girls," said the deejay, over the bank of speakers next to the music console, "the evening's entertainment will be commencing shortly."

There was a cheer and some scattered applause from the audience. Sue and I went to the bar for another drink, and we stopped at the buffet table to fill a couple of plates before we returned to our places. My seat was on the outside of the table, my back to the stage; but if I turned my chair I'd be able to see what was going on. For the moment, I was content to eat and drink.

"Thank you, girls," called the announcer. "I'd like you to give a warm welcome to your friend and his, the one and only . . . Slippery Sammy!"

The cheering and applause was even louder this time, and there were even a few piercing whistles from the crowd. I turned my head, wondering what was going on.

A man appeared on the stage. He was about six foot tall, around twenty-five years old and wearing evening dress. Some kind of singer, I guessed.

Then I heard someone shout, "Look at his balls!"

The remark brought hoots of laughter and loud jeers, and I took a closer look at the man. In one hand he was carrying two balls, the size of tennis balls, and in the other he held a club. A juggler? I could hardly believe it. Was this the kind of entertainment everyone seemed to be awaiting so eagerly?

Sammy took a deep bow, and when he stood up he was holding the two balls and the club against his crotch. Slowly he raised the club towards the vertical in a bizarre imitation of an erect phallus, and he was rewarded with gales of cheers and laughter. I glanced at Sue, and she shrugged disparagingly. I smiled briefly, and she mirrored my expression.

The guy started juggling with the balls and club, while in the background a tape of bland pop music played. He held my interest for about two seconds, then I turned away and studied the audience, amazed by how fascinated they seemed to be in what he was doing. When next I turned around, prompted by a cheer, he had removed his jacket and was ripping off his shirt, tearing away the buttons like Clark Kent about to reveal his secret identity as Superman. But what he did reveal was a broad naked chest, totally hairless, although he still wore his bow tie around his bare neck.

The juggler became a fire-eater. He stepped down from the stage to the middle of the room, and the lights were dimmed as he stroked his arms and chest with burning brands, quenching the flames by thrusting them into his mouth. He strode towards a table on the other side of the room, holding the final flaming rod ahead of him like an Olympic runner, and all those sitting there squealed and leaned away – while everyone else roared with laughter. He kicked his shoes off, running the flickering flames across his bare feet, then thrust the blazing torch into his mouth, exhaling a bright inferno of fire. Cheers and applause followed, and even I clapped my hands in appreciation.

Then he dropped his trousers and stood in the centre of the room clad only in a pair of tight leather shorts which were held together by a criss-cross of laces on each hip. There were more cheers and laughter. The music picked up tempo and volume as he started to dance. He danced across the floor, from table to table, rotating his buttocks and thrusting out his groin. Though I was astounded by some of what he did, I had to admit he was a great athlete. His body was trim, the muscles well toned, and without any apparent effort he could turn cartwheels and somersaults as he flaunted himself at every table. Almost everywhere, hands reached out to stroke his arms or legs, tugging at the ends of the laces in an attempt to tear away his leather shorts.

And finally I realised why they'd all been paying him so much attention earlier: Slippery Sammy was a male stripper!

How far would he go? Female strippers took off everything, I knew, so did that mean he would too? I stared at the other five seated around my table, at their predatory expressions, and I realised that he must strip off totally. That was why everyone was getting so excited.

One row of laces had almost been ripped away, and his shorts were hanging half off as he came to our table. Rose reached out and tweaked one of his nipples, while Jean slapped his almost bare buttock and began tugging at the other laces.

Sammy was standing right next to me when his shorts finally fell away. But he was wearing a kind of thong beneath, a brief cotton pouch which did its best to cover his genitals, and he still had on his incongruous bow tie. He stayed by my side, rocking his hips to and fro at me, slipping his hand inside his tiny garment. I turned away, dimly aware of the uproar which had broken out at the almost total revelation.

I picked up my drink and began sipping at it, trying to move my chair away. But Sammy was holding it down with one of his feet, and I couldn't get away from him. Then Sue reached across and grabbed at the side of the thong, yanking it away – and Sammy's suddenly exposed cock and balls were a few inches from my face! I stared in terrified fascination, unable to close my eyes or look away.

I could hardly believe it. Of all the women in the room, why did he have to choose me?

His was the first adult prick I'd ever seen. It was much longer and fatter than I had imagined. And I thought it looked so ugly and clumsy, not at all beautiful like Carole's cunt. Yet there was something hypnotically attractive about its latent power and raw aggressiveness.

My glass was still held defensively against my mouth. Sammy reached for it and pulled it from my fingers. I watched in horror as he dipped his tool into my drink, stirring it as though it was some huge cocktail stick. I noticed the other girls near me laughing out loud. Then Sammy pulled out his knob and thrust it towards my mouth, spraying alcohol from the end of his cock onto my face. I jerked my head back, but I was still unable to leave my chair; it was as though I'd been tied to it like a torture victim.

He grinned at me, stroking the length of his big pink shaft, and I saw the thing begin to stir of its own accord. He was getting an erection! The whole room erupted in a cacophony of cheering and laughter. I was frozen, wondering what Sammy intended to do next.

Letting go of his half-stiff cock, he jerked his hips up and down at me, while he unfastened his bow tie. He retied it around the middle of his tool, as though it was some ribboned gift. He stepped closer, his penis now horizontal and aimed directly at my mouth.

Distantly, I could hear synchronised clapping, and Sammy was thrusting his cock in time to the audience's enthusiastic beats of applause. Everyone was clapping, even Sue. The swollen purple glans inched its way nearer to me. I started to cry. I hadn't cried for years, but unbidden the tears welled up in my eyes, spilled over and dripped down my cheeks.

It was crazy, but I couldn't help it. Then I reached for my glass where Sammy had replaced it on the table, picked it up and poured my drink all over his offensive weapon. He sprang aside, but I saw he was still grinning as he backed towards the next table. I stood up and walked away, staring at the floor and hoping no one would see my stupid tears.

"Wait!" I recognised the voice behind me as Sue's, and I changed my direction slightly. "Don't go," she begged, catching up with me and putting her hand on my arm.

"Go?" I said, when I reached the bar. "Who's going anywhere? I just want another drink. You didn't really expect me to finish off that glass after he'd washed his dick in it, did you?"

Sue half smiled, but she must have observed my tears and known that I'd been about to leave. "I'll get these," she said, as I ordered my drink. "I could do with another one, too."

We stood at the bar. Sammy was still busy performing for his appreciative audience. He was standing on one of the tables now, while a tall brunette was trying to unfasten his bow tie with her teeth, hampered by the fact that he kept swinging his cock into her face.

"I'm sorry," said Sue. "I didn't think it would be like that."

I shrugged. "It's not your fault," I told her. "I didn't have to come here."

Sue didn't reply. That's when I realised it *was* her fault. This had all been arranged. It wasn't chance that Sammy had picked me out.

She noticed me watching her. "It was only meant to be a bit of fun," she explained. "It happened to me as well, when

I was new here. But it was nothing like this, the way that bastard went for you. I was embarrassed by him suddenly coming up behind me and poking his prick over my shoulder, but not totally humiliated. No, what that guy did just wasn't fair, particularly with you being . . . well . . . you know." She shook her head, watching as Sammy danced nude in the centre of the floor, his penis flopping up and down, beating against his stomach and thighs.

"What am I?" I asked, puzzled.

"You know," Sue answered, glancing around. Then she lowered her voice as though about to utter the most foul obscenity ever deleted from a dictionary. "A virgin."

Her remark threw me a moment. I'd never considered myself a virgin, not after my long affair with Carole, but I supposed that I was.

The others had arranged for Sammy to choose me from the audience, but he'd gone further than they'd expected. And the reason they'd done it was because they thought I was sexually innocent. When it came to men, I was. But that was only a part of the story . . .

There was no harm done, I supposed. The whole incident had only lasted a couple of minutes, and it was kind of funny in a way – now that it was over.

"At least he didn't come all over me," I remarked. "I've just washed my hair."

Sue stared at me in amazement, and I laughed aloud. She smiled and put her arm around my shoulder, hugging me close. She kissed me lightly on the cheek, and I felt the warmth of her breasts against my body. I turned my head swiftly, and her lips briefly brushed against mine. Sue pulled away, her fingers going uncertainly to her mouth.

I knew that was as close as I would ever get to her.

"Does he climax?" I asked, nodding towards Sammy. He was now walking on his hands.

"You've got to be kidding," Sue said. "He doesn't even get it right up. Sex discrimination, isn't it? Wide open cunts in sex magazines for men, but we're not even allowed to see erections. And what good is a dangling prick to anyone?" She glanced at me. "Why do you ask?"

I shrugged.

"He's versatile," Sue commented, when I didn't reply. "Pity he can't do impersonations."

"What do you mean?"

"One of my boyfriends used to do an imitation of a hat stand. He'd hang a hat over the end of his stiffy. He thought it highly amusing."

"Was it?"

"At least it covered up his dick!"

We both laughed.

Then Sue's face became serious again, and she took a gulp from her drink. "I think we ought to do something with Slimy Sam for taking such liberties with you." She nodded her head slowly, watching as he vanished behind the curtains to thunderous applause, cheers and whistles. "I'll go and see the others, find out what they say."

Ten minutes later, Sue and I had made our way to Sammy's dressing room. I knocked on the door. After a few seconds it opened and Sammy peered out. He frowned, then recognised me.

"Hello there," he said. "What can I do for you?"

"It's more what I can do for you," I told him, grinning.

"What *we* can do for you," Sue corrected.

Sammy noticed her for the first time, and he stepped back.

"Come in, come in," he said. "It's always nice to meet my fans." He was wearing a knee-length dressing gown, and he shut the door behind us. It was a small room, with a couch and a single chair the only furniture. He glanced at us expectantly.

"We enjoyed your performance," said Sue.

"That's right," I added. "I'd have liked to respond a bit more to what you were doing earlier, but I'm very shy in public. Maybe I can make up for it now?"

Sammy licked at his lips, glancing at us both, unable to believe his luck. He didn't seem aware of how much he'd upset me before. Perhaps he thought it was only natural we should arrive backstage; maybe this was what usually happened after he'd finished his act.

"Yeah, you really turned us on," said Sue. "My pussy got so hot and wet that I've got to have a few inches of cock sliding into me or else I'll have to frig myself off. So how about it?"

"Both of you?" he asked.

"From what we've seen," said Sue, nodding in the direction of his crotch, "there's plenty for both of us."

I felt very nervous and was letting her do most of the talking; she was the one who had experience of men. Sue was handling it far better than I could, although I was surprised by what she was actually saying to him.

She wore a short green woollen skirt, and she tugged it upwards, flashing her white panties, her hand brushing across her crotch. I saw with delight how prominent was her pubis, noticing a couple of red curls which had escaped from the edge of the tight garment, and my heart began to beat even faster.

"Who do you want first?" Sue asked, letting the skirt fall

back to cover herself and reaching for the belt of Sammy's dressing gown.

He was smiling broadly now, and he let Sue unfasten his belt and pull open his gown. His cock could be seen in the shadows, already beginning to rise.

"How do you manage to keep control out there and not get a total boner?" Sue wanted to know, pulling the dressing gown off his shoulders.

"Trade secret," Sammy smiled, his hand going down to stroke the full length of his stiffening prick.

Sue pushed him towards the couch. "We've got a few secrets, too," she murmured. "You just lie back and we'll show you what I mean. We were worried that you might have jerked yourself off before the performance to keep your prick limp, and you wouldn't have any spunk left for us."

"Don't worry your pretty little head over that," Sammy said, as he lay down.

"I'm not worried," Sue told him, while I opened the door. "You're the one who ought to do the worrying."

Linda and Jean and Rose and Trisha piled into the room, and before Sammy knew what was going on they'd got him pinned down, each seizing an arm or a leg. He tried to struggle, but he couldn't move.

"What's going on?" he demanded, looking worried. He forced a grin. "One at a time girls, hey? Why don't you form a queue outside, hey?"

"Shut up," ordered Sue, and she flicked his dick with her finger.

Sammy shouted out in surprised pain, but as he opened his mouth Sue shoved a wad of tissue inside and he was instantly silent. Then she tied him up, using the belts from his dressing gown and trousers to bind his wrists and ankles to the four corners of the couch. The other girls released their grip. He gazed frantically at us, his eyes wide, his cock wilting.

"You went too far tonight, Sammy," Sue told him, and she glanced at me. "What do we do with him?"

The helpless Sammy was shaking his head desperately from side to side. I felt a bit sorry for him, because he was so weak and powerless when a handful of girls lined up against him. Yet these were the very ones who had arranged for him to pick me out of the audience, so they must share the blame.

I'd already thought up something suitable; Sammy needed to find out what it was like to be on the receiving end of sexual harassment. It was also one way of getting back at the girls, although I'd seen a poster on the wall of the club which had given me another idea of how I might take my revenge against them.

The other five were watching me, waiting, and I smiled a wicked smile.

"I want you to masturbate him," I said.

Each of them looked uneasy at the prospect, and I wasn't sure why this should have been so. They must all have done it for their boyfriends, so what was so different about Sammy? The problem was that they'd probably never done such a thing when there were other girls present, and they felt uncomfortable. But it wasn't as if I was asking them to discard their clothes and fuck him, or even to suck him off. They only had to use their hands.

They knew they owed me this after the stunt they'd pulled, and so reluctantly they went to work.

Sue started first, her fingertips manipulating Sammy's shrunken organ, and I envied him her attention. But she met with little success, because he was so scared.

"Come on, help me," she said to the others. "We've got to work on his whole body."

So the rest of them joined in, stroking the supine Sammy's legs and thighs, his face and neck, his arms and nipples, and gradually his penis began to rise and become rigid. Sue let go, and Linda took over, working against his length with the clenched fist of her right hand, fondling his testicles with the fingers of her left. Then it was Jean's turn, and she wet her palm with saliva and concentrated on the tip of Sammy's knob, sliding the foreskin to and fro with short rapid strokes.

I tried to watch disinterestedly, although I could feel my labia becoming moist with sexual excitement. I tried to tell myself this was because of watching the girls in action, but I wasn't convinced. It was Sammy's hardness which was the centre of my attention, and I began to wonder what it would be like to have a cock thrusting into me . . .

Soon after Rose had taken the helm, the lucky penis began to twitch of its own volition. There were only a few spurts, the first of which squirted several creamy drops of semen three or four inches onto Sammy's chest. Then a couple more sticky drops oozed from the tip, onto his stomach and slowly ran down towards his hips and dripped on the couch.

And that was it. I wasn't very impressed; it seemed I hadn't been missing much.

Rose wiped her fingers on Sammy's leg, and Trisha looked relieved that she hadn't been forced to lend such an intimate hand. They and the others made for the door.

I stood by Sammy's side, staring down at him. He didn't seem too happy in his post-orgasmic rapture and was watching me cautiously, wondering what was going to happen to him next. I looked at his deflated organ, and I noticed a pool of semen in his navel.

It was the first time I'd seen spunk, but there had been a lot of firsts today. The first time I'd seen a penis so closely; the first erection I'd watched; the first male climax I'd witnessed.

Tentatively, I reached out my right index finger, dipping it into the creamy drops of come. The stuff felt warm, and I rubbed it between my finger and thumb, studying the slimy texture and the way it clung to my skin.

I shook my head slowly as if in disappointment, then backed away and headed for the door.

" 'Bye, Sammy," I called, turning and blowing him a farewell kiss. "Nice to have seen you." I made sure the door was ajar so that someone would find him.

As I went down the steps towards the exit, I took another look at the notice I'd seen earlier.

FIVE

"I'd like to see The Castle again under different circumstances," I said on Monday morning, when we were all taking our coffee break. "Why don't we go again this Friday, the six of us? I don't think Sammy will be there."

"It'll be a long time before he shows his face again," said Rose.

"Or anything else!" added Sue, and we all laughed.

"I feel a bit bad about what happened to him," I said. "After all, he was only doing his job."

"Don't feel sorry for him," Jean told me. "He loved it. He got more out of it than we did. It'll make a great story for him to tell his friends, how he was stripped and tossed off by six girls."

"That's right," Trisha agreed. "If you pay as much attention to a guy's cock as you do to the rest of his body, you can't go wrong." She was looking at me as she spoke, offering me sisterly advice on how to keep a man.

"Yeah," nodded Linda. "That's why the first thing they try to do is shove a couple of fingers up your honey pot. They think they're doing you a favour, because there's nothing they like better than a hand on their dick. They're so used to giving themselves a manual, you see."

I could tell they all felt guilty for what had happened to me on Friday, although I was no longer bothered. But they couldn't bring themselves to make an explicit apology, and so they were doing it in a circuitous way. I'd never heard them talk so frankly about sex before. As I listened, I nodded my head even though I knew that I'd never benefit from their knowledge and experience . . .

"So what about Friday?" I asked.

"I've got a date," said Rose.

"Me too," said Trisha.

"Bring them along," I suggested. "The more the merrier. We'll have a party. You can all bring a man along, I don't mind. I just want to go back to The Castle again, because I think I might like it this time." I really rubbed it in, making them feel even worse about the other night. I stared at Sue, looking for some support.

She glanced at Linda, who nodded, and one by one the others agreed.

"Good," I said, smiling. But none of them knew why I was smiling.

On Friday evening, we all met up at The Castle once more. We were in a different room, a larger one, because it wasn't a private party this time. All of the others had brought a boyfriend, and that made it even better. I felt a twinge of jealousy when I saw the man sitting next to Sue, his hand casually resting on her bare knee. Sue introduced us, his name was Philip, and he went and bought me a drink.

"So here we are," Sue said. "Happy now?"

I nodded, glancing around so that I didn't meet her eye, instead focusing on the people dancing near the stage. Sue seemed aware that something wasn't quite right, although clearly she had no idea what it was. None of the others seemed suspicious. I'd been concerned that they would have seen signs or posters proclaiming tonight's special attraction, but the only thing which might give a clue was the red and white banner which hung over the stage at the end of the room. It was the name of the drinks company which was sponsoring the event.

Some of the others at our table joined the dancers or went to the bar for more drinks, but I simply sat and waited. Finally the music stopped and an announcer appeared.

"Good evening, ladies and gentlemen," he said. "I'm sorry to interrupt the music, but this concerns five ladies who I believe are in the audience and should be backstage." He pulled a piece of paper from one of the pockets of his dinner jacket. "Are these girls here?" he asked, glancing around the crowded room. Then he read out Linda's, Rose's, Trisha's, Sue's and Jean's names.

I was watching their mystified expressions, as they automatically answered him.

"Come on then, ladies," the announcer said, beckoning to them. Hesitantly, they stood up. "The Wet T-shirt Contest starts in ten minutes. You've got to get changed."

They froze immediately, staring at each other and their escorts, while some of the audience clapped and cheered them. The five of them and their boyfriends all started talking at once, arguing and protesting.

"Come on, come on," called the compere, impatiently.

Linda shook her head frantically. "There's some kind of mistake," she claimed.

Rose sat down quickly, Trisha's man pulled her back into her seat, Jean took a few backward steps as though the announcer intended to drag her forcibly up onto the stage . . . and Sue glanced at me.

I sat without moving, trying to look innocent. But I couldn't keep my face straight, and I put my glass to my mouth to try and mask my smile.

"It was you!" Sue accused me. "You put our names down!"

"Me?" I said, frowning. "I don't know what you're talking about." Then I burst out laughing, and they all stared at me. "You should have seen your faces!" I shook my head in amusement.

Sue sat down. "Very funny," she said, nodding her head resignedly. She leaned towards Philip, telling him what was going on and briefly explaining why I must have done it. The other girls glared at me.

"Come on, ladies," said the announcer. He watched as Jean, the last of the five, took her seat again. "Don't be shy. We're all waiting for you."

Philip angrily shouted, "They're not coming!"

The compere came down from the stage, striding towards our table. He stared at the girls, his hands on his hips. "What do you mean?" he demanded.

"There's been a mistake," said Linda. "I told you that."

"It's all a joke," Sue explained. "Someone's been playing a practical joke."

The announcer couldn't absorb this information. He held out the piece of paper towards them. "These are your names, aren't they?"

"That's right," Rose's boyfriend said. "But none of them are entering your fucking stupid contest, so fuck off."

"But . . ." The compere was about about forty years old, his hair combed sideways in a failed attempt to hide his baldness. He sighed, then leaned forward on the table, lowering his voice. "Without them, there'll be no contest," he said, staring at the men as though the girls weren't there. "These five are half the entrants. There's a minimum entry of six, it's in the company rules. So the whole thing will be off." He glanced around the room. "And there'll be a lot of disappointed people here. I wouldn't like to be in your shoes tonight. There could be trouble."

"Tough shit," said Trisha's man, putting her arm defensively around her shoulder.

"You've already got five girls, right?" said Sue. "So you only need one more?"

"Yes!" agreed the compere. "Just one of you." He studied each of the five in turn. "Please?" Licking at his dry lips, he added, "Look, we can come to some financial arrangement if that's what it takes." He looked optimistically towards Sue, hoping she was going to volunteer.

"She's not going on that stage," warned Philip.

Sue glanced at him, pushing his hand off her arm. "What I do, or don't do, is up to me," she told him coldly. Then she levelled her expressionless eyes at me.

I wasn't sure what a Wet T-shirt Contest involved, and when I'd put their names forward I hadn't expected any of them to enter. I just wanted some measure of revenge for the previous week's escapade, but I hadn't anticipated that it would cause all this bother.

"I'll do it," I said quietly, under Sue's mesmerising gaze. I regretted my rash words nearly at once, but it was too late. The announcer grabbed my arm and almost lifted me out of my chair. As if in a dream, I shrugged his hand off and walked towards the stage. None of this was real, it couldn't be happening.

Almost before I realised it, I was behind the curtains and the compere was talking to me.

"I'm Tony," he said, "and I really appreciate this. And if I appreciate it, then the company appreciates it. There's a lot of money riding on these promotions. What's your name? How old are you? How much do you want for this?"

I answered his first questions but couldn't think of a reply to the third. So Tony named a sum. It was as much as I earned in a week.

"Yes," I said, and I nodded my head.

"Good girl," he grabbed my wrist and pulled me to a door. "Now go and get changed."

"Into what?"

"It's all in there. Is there anything you want? A drink?"

I nodded again.

"Good, fine, good."

Then he was gone, and I found myself behind the door and in a changing room. I stared at the unbelievable sight which confronted me: the five other contestants, half-dressed, half-naked. It was this which brought me back to awareness. I gazed at the beautiful nude female flesh, which reminded me what I'd been missing since I'd lost Carole.

One girl was totally naked, with high conical breasts and a trimmed thatch of brown pubic hair; another displayed the most gorgeous backside; a couple of the others were topless, while the last was only wearing a T-shirt which ended just above a neat triangle of black curls.

A Wet T-shirt Contest. Did that mean wearing absolutely nothing but a white T-shirt, which was emblazoned with the name of the drinks company in bright red letters across the breasts? Surely it couldn't do.

But whatever it was, as I gazed at the other girls I was certainly glad I'd come here. My nipples hardened and I felt a throbbing deep within my crotch.

Then the door opened again, and a smartly dressed woman appeared. "There you are," she said to me. "Get your clothes off, put these on."

I looked at what she'd given me, a pair of white shorts and

T-shirt. I did what I was told, because I wanted to stay in this room with the other five barely clad females.

Stripping down to my skimpy briefs, I watched the girls. None of them spared me more than a glance. They were all dressed now in their uniform of tight shorts and even tighter T-shirts, looking more like athletes than entrants in some nightclub contest – although their high-heeled shoes would have been out of place on a running track. As I donned my T-shirt, I wondered vaguely why they used the word "wet" in the title, but my thoughts were on other matters. I was here now and had to make the most of it, and I began to pull on my shorts.

The woman organiser came over to me. "A word of advice," she said. "You'd do better without your panties, because the line shows through your shorts."

I'd noticed that none of the others wore a bra beneath their T-shirts, presumably for the same reason. Taking off the shorts again, I thumbed down my briefs, then pulled my shorts on once more, tugging them up and stroking my palm against my cunt as if admiring the snug fit, but in reality pressing my middle finger against my labia to give myself a moment of pleasure.

The door opened once more. It was Tony, carrying a tray laden with glasses. He passed them around to the contestants, giving another to the woman and saving the final one for himself. It was the same stuff we were advertising on our T-shirts.

"Okay, girls," he said, looking us all up and down. "The rules are very simple. I'll announce you one at a time, and you come onto the stage. When you go off again, the next girl follows on immediately. I gauge the audience reaction, the applause, and the best three will come back again. The audience picks the winner. It's as simple as that. The winner goes through to the national finals with a chance for the grand prize, but you all get a free bottle of . . ." He held up his glass, raised it in a toast to us all. "Relax. You don't have to do anything. It's all in fun." He took a sip of his drink. "And may the best girl win."

He was standing next to one of the other girls, and as he turned to leave I saw her hand reach out to touch his groin with a lingering caress. That couldn't have done much harm to her chances, I realised.

"I'll send you out one by one," the woman organiser said, as she stood in the doorway, facing towards the stage and watched for the signal. "Right, Candy, off you go."

Candy was the girl I'd seen totally nude, and she hurried from the room. Before long, we heard a huge cheer drift through from the audience. Then the second girl was called.

Finally there were only two of us left, the other being the one who'd rubbed the compere's crotch. She was about the same height as me, with short auburn hair. Although her hips were wider than mine, her boobs were about the same size, but more droopy.

"Joanne," said the woman, and Joanne disappeared through the doorway.

Now that I was alone, I picked up the other glasses which hadn't been drained, tipping the contents down my throat in record time. I heard Joanne's cheer, and then it was my turn.

I didn't feel nervous at all as I walked out onto the stage. It was simply one of those things which had to be done, and worrying about it wouldn't make it any better. At least I could console myself with the thought of the money Tony had promised me, then I wondered if there was any way I could be certain I'd be paid.

I took no notice of the audience, hardly heard what Tony was saying as he walked me to the centre of the stage. There was no sign of the other girls, who had gone off the stage at the other side. What puzzled me most was that the floor was all wet.

Tony stepped back, and I became aware off a photographer standing on the main floor a couple of yards away, his camera aimed at me.

Then Tony hurled a bucket of cold water all over me!

I staggered back in surprise, too astonished even to cry out. At last I became aware of the significance of the contest's name. The water had been aimed at my T-shirt, although my face and legs had also been splashed. But my shirt was soaked through, and it clung tightly to the contours of my body, showing every detail of my breasts. The coldness of the water had stiffened my nipples even more, and their rigid outlines and colour stood out through the thin fabric which had become almost transparent.

The audience cheered and whistled and clapped, while the photographer clicked away. I wiped some drops of water from my face, and watched them all, then turned towards Tony who was dutifully applauding me. I guessed it was my own ignorance which had led me into this and that the others had known what they were letting themselves in for.

Tony took me around the waist and hustled me backstage, to where the other five were waiting.

"Okay," he said, and he pointed to Candy and Joanne. "You, you." He nodded to me. "And you. You're the finalists. The rest of you, go through there and get changed. Thank you very much." He glanced at the three of us who were left. "Same as before, okay? More water to get you nice and—" he licked his lips "—moist. Only this time you stay on stage, so we end up with all three of you together. Don't forget to smile. Ready?"

"Yes," said Candy, and she gave both her nipples a squeeze. They needed it, not being very prominent.

I nodded. So did Joanne – and a moment later Tony stroked her curvy bottom. Then he went back onto the stage, calling us up one by one. I listened as the other two were drenched and cheered in turn. As Tony called my name, something attracted my attention. There was a spare bucket of water near where I stood.

I picked up the bucket and began to carry it towards the stage, picking up momentum as I heard my name called again. Then I dashed on the stage, saw the other two girls, saw Tony – and I flung all the water at him! I caught him squarely on the head and chest as he tried to duck. He backed away and stepped out of sight, and I became aware that the cheers and laughter were far louder than they had been all evening.

Candy and Joanne watched me with amazement. My run had carried me past them and to the water which had been prepared for me. I discarded the empty bucket and lifted the other one, wondering what to do. From the corner of my eye, I saw Tony. He stepped further into the shadows when he noticed what I was holding.

I stepped to the edge of the stage, and began to swing the bucket, watching the looks of dismay from the people sitting in the front tables as they threw up their arms and leaned away, thinking I was going to hurl the water all over them. But instead I raised the bucket high into the air, then tilted it, pouring the contents all over myself, soaking my hair, drenching my clothes, wetting every inch of my skin–and relishing the gales of applause from the audience.

Then Tony appeared by my side, taking the empty bucket from my hands. He wasn't quite as wet as I was, although water dripped from his no longer combed-over hair. He glared at me as he put the bucket down and spoke into his microphone.

"Ladies and gentlemen," he said, wiping his face with his sleeve, "I have great pleasure in announcing that the winner of tonight's heat of the Wet T-shirt Contest is . . . me!" He paused to allow the burst of laughter. "No, seriously, ladies and gentlemen, tonight's contest has been very close – not to say unusual. I think they all ought to win, and they've each won an entry in my address book already, but the third place goes to . . . Candy!"

Candy accepted her applause, and left the stage at the compere's nod. Tony came to stand between me and Joanne. It was obvious who ought to have won: my soaking wet outfit proved beyond any doubt that I had a much better figure than Joanne's. And the audience had already given me the biggest cheers of the night for my performances with the two buckets. But it was equally evident to me which of us Tony wanted to win.

"This is going to be tough," he told everyone. "I think you ought to remind me just how good you think our two beautiful finalists are. How about another big cheer for Joanne?"

I noticed him prod her in the ribs with his elbow. Joanne glanced at him doubtfully, but he nodded. Her applause was beginning to fade – until she suddenly took off her T-shirt and stood topless, raising her arms to lift her breasts. The clapping and cheering were renewed, doubling in volume and intensity, finally dying away.

Then Tony called on my supporters to show their appreciation.

A voice in the crowd shouted out, "Strip!"

More people took up the word, turning it into a chant: "Strip, strip, strip!" They began clapping in unison as they yelled for me to disrobe.

I stared out into the audience, searching for Sue's face, because what I did next was for her: I peeled off my dripping T-shirt, swirling it around my head and then flinging it into the audience. They shouted and clapped and whistled even louder, with far more enthusiasm than they'd given Joanne.

I stood with my arms raised and turned to one side to show my profile – my boobs' profile, of course. But I kept on turning until my back was to the crowd, and I swung my hips from side to side in time to the background music. I slipped my thumbs into my waistband and slowly, slowly, slid down my shorts. The applause increased. I let my shorts fall and I was naked.

Then I spun around. Hands on hips, my feet braced twenty inches apart, wearing nothing but my shoes, I faced a massed throng of strangers. And they went wild.

Needless to say, I won. Joanne wasn't prepared to go to the same lengths as me. Although I'd stripped off for Sue, she'd never know it, and it was the males in the audience who vented their approval of my display and voted me so noisily into first place.

My nude body glinted with drops of water as I raised my arms above my head, clenching my hands together in a victory salute.

And as I stood there, revelling in their enthusiastic response, I closed my eyes, clenching the muscles of my cunt to trigger off the first orgasm I'd ever had without some sort of physical stimulation. It was though everyone in the crowd had been fucking me, all the men, all the girls, because it was they who had stimulated me – just by being there and reacting so positively to my body.

For a moment, as I spiralled higher and higher, then closed my legs to prolong the spasms, I wondered about the effect that my nude body must have been having on the watching males, aware that I was being carried aloft by their combined sexual power.

Then I felt something being draped over my shoulder, and I opened my eyes as Tony hung the winner's sash across me. He used the opportunity to stroke the palm of his hand across my right breast, while the fingers of his other hand brushed against my pubic hairs as he pretended to adjust the sash. It was the first time a man had touched me in either place, and because I was still trembling in the last internal throes of orgasm I didn't mind. It was worse when he kissed my cheek a minute later, after making a short speech which I wasn't listening to. He presented me with a bottle of spirits, and I wiped my cheek with the back of my hand.

I was watching the crowd as I slowly recovered from my few seconds of ecstasy. It wasn't the best orgasm I'd ever had, but it was by no means the least memorable.

I could hardly believe what had occurred, from the moment I'd volunteered to join the contest right up until that instant, but I wouldn't have missed it for anything. The sash didn't hide my vital assets from view, hanging as it did between my breasts and over one hip.

While I gazed at the crowd, I saw the photographer again. He was still taking pictures of me. I wasn't sure I approved of that. What I'd done had been totally spontaneous, and it ought to be soon forgotten, but photographs would provide a permanent record of my temporary lunacy.

"Okay," whispered Tony in my ear. "They've all had a

good look. Let's go before you catch cold." He took my wrist and led me off the stage, although I turned and waved my prize bottle and was rewarded with a final cheer.

"You were great, girl," Tony said, as we headed for the dressing room. "That must have been one of the best contests ever. Keep it up and you could win the final." I felt his hand slide down my back towards my bare buttocks.

I spun around angrily. "Take your hands off me!" I ordered. "Just because I won, doesn't mean I've become your prize. And I've no intention of entering any more of these stupid competitions."

He stared at me as though I was talking a foreign language, and he paused halfway through opening the door. I pushed my way in, slamming the door on him. He tried to follow me, but the woman official was there and she refused to admit him.

Pulling off my sash, I dropped it on the floor then walked to the bench where I'd left my clothes. The other girls were almost dressed by now, and they watched me.

"Congratulations," said one. "That took a lot of nerve."

"Yes," another agreed. "I wouldn't have dared do it."

"Maybe I would," Candy said, "if I looked as good as you. You've got a fantastic body, you know."

I nodded, not in answer but more in thanks for what they'd said.

Joanne was staring at me. "Well done," she muttered, making no attempt to disguise her lack of sincerity.

"That was quite daring," said the woman, bringing me a towel as I sat down. "I'm still nervous about undressing when my husband's in the room, but in front of all those people . . ." She shook her head in admiration, then she began to dry my hair for me.

The number of people hadn't bothered me. When there were so many, it was hard to think of them as individuals. I'd only been concerned about one person in the audience, and that had been Sue. But I realised now that my action had been a mistake; she wouldn't understand my motivation. There would never be anything between us. I could accept it logically, but not emotionally. The only solution was not to go back to work at the office, or else Sue would always be there to remind me of what was so near but so far. I'd have to leave, find another job. At least I had the promise of some money from Tony. After my performance tonight, he could hardly go back on his word, although he might object if I remained determined not to enter the final.

If those drinks I'd had could make me behave like that, then plenty of guys would be buying some for their girls tonight. But of course it hadn't simply been the alcohol, although I could use that as an excuse.

It surprised me what the woman said about me being so daring. The most daring part had been going on stage; that was something which would always have scared me previously. Anyone who was up in front of hundreds of people, all of them watching their every move, had to be brave as far as I was concerned. Taking one's clothes off is the simplest thing in the world. It's clothes which are so unnatural. Humans aren't born fully dressed, it's civilisation which demands that we must wear clothing.

If it weren't for the whims of the climate, I think I'd prefer to be nude all the time. I like dressing up and wearing the latest fashions as much as any woman, but I feel much more free when undressed. People are more honest and open when they can't hide behind their clothes, pretending to be something which they aren't. All men are born free, says an ancient slogan, to which should be added that they are also born naked. Only when we're all nude can there ever be any equality. Who would be in such reverential awe of presidents and politicians, of kings and dictators, if they were naked? But that's what the famous fairy tale, The Emperor's New Clothes, is all about.

"You must be pleased with your prize," the woman said, bringing me back to the present. I opened my eyes. She was still towelling my damp hair. I'd been allowing my thoughts to drift, pretending that I was back with Carole again. "A new hairdo at the town's best salon, and a new outfit from the top boutique."

I sighed. So much for nudity.

"And then there's the final," she continued. "First prize is a round-the-world holiday."

I pulled gently away from her and began to get dressed, my body was almost dry by now.

"I've had enough of wet T-shirts," I said. "I don't think I could do it again."

"But you have to," the woman insisted. "It's in the rules. The winner of each heat has to go through to the finals." She lowered her voice, glancing at Joanne who was combing her hair. "If you refuse, you lose tonight's first place."

I shrugged, not caring, and finished dressing. I wondered what to do now, not fancying returning to the table with the others. All the guys would be staring at me, grinning and joking. I didn't mind them looking from a distance, when they were just faces in a crowd, but I wouldn't like them to get too close. Okay, so I'd taken my clothes off. But that didn't mean I was available for the first cock that came along. Or any cock.

But Tony seemed to think he was first in line. When the

other girls had gone and the organiser also left for a minute, he marched into the dressing room, smiling what he thought was an irresistible smile. He'd changed into a smart casual suit, and though his hair was still damp it was combed back into place.

"And how's the most beautiful girl I've ever seen in or out of a wet T-shirt?" he wanted to know, leaning forward and trying to kiss my cheek again.

I managed to evade his lunge, ducking away and stepping aside. "Do me a favour, will you?" I asked.

"For you," he said, "anything."

"Fuck off."

Tony stopped dead in his tracks, as though he couldn't believe his ears.

"You tell him, sweetie," I heard another voice say, and I looked around to see the photographer leaning against the wall by the door. He was watching us both.

"Keep out of this, George," warned Tony, turning his attention to me again.

"When do I get this money you promised me?" I demanded.

"We'll sort that out over dinner," Tony said. "Do you like Greek food?"

"I like Greek," interrupted George, holding up his camera and pretending to take a shot of Tony being annoyed. But I could see the cover was across the lens.

"Get out of here, George!" snapped Tony, impatiently.

"Why?"

"George, I'm warning you!"

"What are you going to do," George asked, throwing up his hands in mock fear. "Hit me? Oh, go on, please. You're so manly, so tough, so virile."

Tony grimaced, trying to keep his temper. "What is it you want, George?"

"I want to talk to this young lady," came the reply. "And unlike you, that's all I want."

I glanced from one to the other, not really wishing to talk to either of them; but I wanted my money from one and a roll of film from the other.

"This is business, Tony," said George. "Company business."

"I'm talking business, too," Tony said, defensively. "We've got to sort out the finals."

"That's all routine, you know it. If you've come to some private arrangement, you can work that out later when I'm not here."

"All he's got to work out," I said, speaking up at last, "is the money he promised me for being the sixth contestant. That's the only arrangement we've got."

"In which case," George told Tony, "I suggest you go and get the girl's money."

Tony opened his mouth to speak, then thought better of it. He nodded his head and quickly walked towards the door.

"She'll still be here when you come back," George assured him. "We're not going to elope." He chuckled far more than this remark deserved. "I don't blame you, sweetie," he said to me, making sure Tony could hear him. "He's not my type either."

I stared at him suspiciously. "Why were you taking my photograph before? I didn't say you could." I held out my hand. "I'd like the film."

"Ha!" he snorted. "That's a good one, I must remember it." He sat down on the bench, looking up at me and pulling a packet of cigarettes from his jacket pocket. He was in his mid-thirties, over six feet tall, very thin, almost like a skeleton covered with skin; he wore thick-lensed glasses with wire rims; his curly hair was as blonde as my own, but from his dark complexion it had to be bleached; and he was dressed all in denim – jeans, open-necked shirt, jacket. When I declined his offer of a cigarette, he lit one with a match, inhaled, then blew a cloud of hazy smoke out of the corner of his mouth. All the time his eyes were studying me.

I waited for him to continue speaking, and finally he did.

"These photographs," he said, tapping his camera with the hand which held the cigarette, "are the property of the company. Because you were in the contest, they own the copyright in those photographs of you."

"What happens to them?"

He shrugged. "They get pinned to the walls of the management washroom so that the executives can toss themselves off while looking at them," he told me.

"What?"

He grinned. "Would that bother you?"

I thought about it for a few seconds. Why should it bother me? I shrugged.

"No, they use them for publicity," George said. "All those boobs with the company name stuck to them, it's the image they want: drink their booze and you get laid. Though I doubt if any of yours can be used, the nude ones, because they don't have the logo on them. Pity."

"The name was on the sash," I reminded him. There was no harm in pointing that out. He'd realise when he developed the photos.

He nodded thoughtfully, still watching me. "Anyhow," he said, "as you've guessed, I work for the company. I'm freelance, which is why that jerk Tony can't fire me. If he makes trouble, he's the one who's replaceable, not me." He took another deep drag. "And I think we could hit it off together, you and I."

I took half a step backwards, but George shook his head rapidly.

"No, not like that, sweetie," he told me. "You aren't my type either, I'm afraid."

For a moment I didn't understand, then suddenly I did. George meant that he was homosexual. I'd never met one before. He seemed like anyone else. But so did I, I supposed. I hardly thought of myself as lesbian, but I was. In a way I had more in common with George than I did with most other girls.

He must have noticed the dawning realisation in my eyes, because he nodded and said, "I know I'm a great disappointment to you, sweetie, that you were just itching to have my throbbing steel-like knob pounding into your tight juicy quim."

I laughed, and so did he.

"But it's true that all I want you for is your body," he continued. "How do you fancy doing some modelling work?"

"For this lot?" I asked, kicking at the sash with my foot.

"To start with, yes. There's a project which might interest you. But there's all sorts of possibilities. You're obviously not shy about your body."

"So you mean nude photographs?"

"Blondes are so rare," George said, nodding and twisting a lock of his own hair between his fingers. "Real blondes, which you've already proved you are. What do you say?"

I said nothing, because I was thinking. I'd already decided I had to find another job, and the idea was tempting.

"There's a lot of money to be made if you're successful," George added. "You've got wonderful bone structure, and you're the right shape for a fashion model if you want to move in that direction. The top ones make a fortune and screw movie stars and rock musicians."

"Don't tell me the disadvantages," I said, grinning.

George frowned for a moment, then shrugged. He dropped his cigarette on the floor and ground it out beneath his sole. "What do you say?" he repeated.

Before I could say anything, Tony was back in the room, an envelope in one hand. He ignored George, giving me the envelope. I opened it up.

"It's all there," he assured me.

I counted out the notes, and it was. "Thanks," I said. I looked up. "Why don't you take me for a drink?"

Tony straightened. He smiled confidently as he preened himself, dusting down the collar of his jacket.

"I'd love to, sweetie," replied George, who was the one I'd been looking at. "But just one, I don't want you getting me tipsy and taking unfair advantage of my body."

Tony watched dumbly as George and I walked out of the dressing room together.

SIX

After George had filled my head with his glamorous talk of travelling the world as a model, I decided that I might as well enter the final of the Wet T-Shirt Contest. Now that I had no job, the first prize was very tempting. And even if I came last, my fare to the city and hotel expenses were all paid for.

The final was a far more sedate affair than the heat which I'd won, because we were given strict instructions not to strip off. Even our T-shirts had to be kept on. Obviously the judges had never seen any bare boobs before, and no one wished to offend them.

Three judges had been appointed: the chairman of the company, a television actor and a famous footballer. Or at least he was meant to be famous, although I'd never heard of him. There could be no fiddling with the results this time, or so I thought, because Tony was no longer the sole arbiter of audience reaction.

But gauging the audience's response would have been the fairest system, or perhaps I'd have thought differently had I won. Instead, I came third. The girl who was placed second went off with the actor, and I saw the winner climbing into a chauffeured limousine with the company chairman. Probably it was my role to be awarded to the not so famous football player, but I managed to evade him.

Third prize was a useful amount of cash, equivalent to three months' pay where I used to work, so I'd done pretty well out of the liquor company. I still hadn't touched the bottle which all the contestants had received the first night, a month before. I'd considered giving it to the girls in the office as a farewell present; but there was no farewell, because after the contest I simply never went back there.

When I'd finished dressing after the final, George was waiting for me. It was the first time we'd met since going for a drink together, when he'd talked about modelling. I'd noticed him earlier, out in front of the stage, his camera working overtime.

"Hello, sweetie," he said. "Sorry you didn't win."

"I didn't fancy the first prize," I told him.

"The chairman?"

I nodded.

"I know what you mean," said George. "I preferred that footballer myself. I really go for the sporty types." He licked lasciviously at his lips, and I laughed.

"Who needs a trip around the world when you've promised me fame and fortune?" I asked.

"You've thought over what I said?" George nodded in answer to his own question. "That's good. Let's go for the most expensive meal in town. The company's paying, and we can discuss it."

Which was what we did, going to a very swish restaurant for the most lavish meal I'd ever consumed in my life. If George ate in such a fashion all the time, I couldn't understand why he was so slim. A couple of meals like that each week and I'd soon lose my figure. We talked about all sorts of things, and I was able to relax and enjoy myself in George's company because there was no sexual pressure on me. It was only at the end of the meal that we finally began to discuss photography and modelling.

"I'll need to take some test shots of you for a portfolio to show the marketing people," George said, as we sat with our coffee and liqueurs. "We can do that tomorrow if you haven't got anything planned."

"Only sightseeing," I said. "I've never been here before. So it's all new and exciting. It makes where I come from seem so dull and outdated."

George shrugged. "I've lived here all my life, so I prefer it when I go to small towns. They're not so cold and inhospitable, they've got more character." He shrugged again. "I suppose it depends what you're used to. The grass is always greener somewhere else, they say. And speaking of somewhere else, have you ever been to the Caribbean?"

"You must be kidding," I laughed. "I've never even been out of the country."

"Then you'd better get yourself a passport. Fast. Because I'm flying out to the Caribbean next week. And you're coming with me."

I laughed again, but George didn't. I studied his expression and I could tell that he was serious.

"You mean it, don't you?" I said.

He nodded, draining his coffee and then lighting a cigarette.

I waited impatiently for him to finish this ritual. "Are you going to explain what you mean," I asked, "or do I have to guess?"

"You're going to become a calendar girl, sweetie. Does that appeal to you?"

"Tell me more," I insisted.

"The company issues a calendar every year," George explained. "It's sent out free to all their customers, clubs and bars and retailers all over the world. This time the location is the Caribbean. I'm the photographer, and we're taking four girls. I've already signed up three photographic models and I want you to be the fourth. There was some talk of the winner of tonight's contest being given the job, but I can fix that. What do you say?"

"What's the catch?"

"You get flown to a Caribbean island, stay in a luxury hotel, go swimming, diving, surfing, paragliding, jet-skiing, sunbathing, while I take photographs of you. You get paid a lot of money."

"What's the catch?" I repeated.

"It's hard work, it's boring."

"You ever tried working in an office?" I asked.

"So you'll say 'yes'?"

There was something wrong here. It sounded far too good to be true. I twirled my empty glass between my fingers, wondering why George really wanted me to go. I couldn't think of an answer, so I asked him.

"Why do you really want me to go?"

"So that when you're famous and successful, you'll be able to say it was old George who discovered you." He laughed disparagingly. "No? Well, it's because I want to do a good job on this calendar, and you match exactly my vision for the project. It's as simple as that. Just tit and bum. No crotch shots, it isn't the right image for the company."

"I'm not bothered about that." I'd got over my earlier resentment of George taking those nude pictures of me, because what was a photograph after all? It was only a piece of paper.

"Then what's the problem? The Caribbean is fabulous, that's why I chose it."

"You chose it?"

"The company thinks they chose it, and they think they picked the girls for the trip. They'll also think that you were their choice. It's hard work, but it's fun. Come on, sweetie, all you have to do is say 'yes'."

"Yes," I said.

Ten days later I was lying on a white Caribbean beach wearing nothing but the brief lower half of a bikini, sipping at an iced glass of the product we were promoting while George took my photograph. It looked an ideal scene, all alone on the burning sand. But as well as George, a dozen other people were clustered around me.

All of them were involved in producing the pictures for the calendar. I'd imagined that it would be just George and the models flying out to the island. But that was only the beginning. George had an assistant, and the assistant had an assistant. There was a guy to handle the lights, even under the brilliant sunlight we needed lights, and he had an assistant. There was a girl for our hair, a girl for our make-up, a girl for our costumes. Hers must have been the easiest job of all because of how little we wore.

A few times we'd have visitors, a representative from the advertising agency or the company would appear for a few hours then fly back again. They must have spent a fortune simply to come up with twelve pictures. Simply? Nothing was simple, I learned. The schedule worked out at less than one completed photograph a day. But to get that final dozen for the calendar, George shot hundreds of rolls of film.

I'd been lying in almost the same position for hours, my body shaded from the blazing sun by a huge parasol, while George took endless photos and my glass was refilled again and again. Not because I'd been drinking the stuff, but because the ice kept melting in the heat. And all the while I had to look as though I was having the time of my life.

The other three girls were professional models, although I discovered that the one called Vanessa had only been working as such for three months. They all had suntans from recent work in the Mediterranean and Australia; they had to be careful always to sunbathe nude, because a bikini line would lose them work. I had no such problem, my skin being equally pale all over at first. Whenever they had the opportunity, the other three stripped off completely. And soon so did I.

They had no inhibitions about anyone seeing them naked. The only similar experience I'd had was in the first Wet T-shirt Competition, but those circumstances had been unusual and I'd also been a bit drunk that night. I soon got used to the calendar crew watching me as I posed. But it took longer to ignore the stares of complete strangers, passers-by who might only be a few yards away.

The other two girls were Sandra and Debbie, and I got on very well with them all. At first I thought they'd resent me as an outsider, but they were full of help and advice, as though we four were allies against the rest of the team.

The three of them were so gorgeous and attractive that I couldn't understand why I'd been chosen to join them. Evidently George saw something in me that I wasn't aware of at the time, and it was an honour to be considered in the same class as the other three. Sandra, Debbie and Vanessa were the most beautiful girls I'd ever met. They looked good from every angle. They didn't need make-up or elaborate hair styles – or clothes. They were models because of their perfection. Their faces and figures were their fortunes

Naturally enough I fell in love again. This time it was with Debbie. Or, to be more precise, I fell in love with her cunt.

Debbie was a tall willowy girl with high thrusting breasts

and jet black hair which hung halfway down her back. But her cunt was completely hairless, and the first time she stripped off in front of me I couldn't keep my eyes off her brazen crotch. It looked so beautiful and tasty I had to restrain myself from licking my lips, but there was no way that I could prevent my inner labia beginning to swell and moisten at such a marvellous sight. Some day, I resolved, I'd shave my own twat.

That was the first night we arrived, and she and I were sharing a room. Debbie had just had a shower and couldn't fail to notice where my attention was directed. She glanced at herself, lightly touching her smooth mound.

"It turns a lot of men on," she confided.

I could well imagine that it did, because it was certainly turning me on.

"Is that why you did it?" I asked.

"Not originally. I was getting my bikini line done, ready for a shoot, and on impulse I asked the girl for a complete wax."

"Ouch," I said, wincing.

"I've had it like this for a long time," she added, "and quite a few guys have told me that it's better than getting hairs in their mouth." She smiled as she remembered. "But I've got to insist that they have a close shave, too, or else their bristles can be quite painful."

I began to undress for the shower, then slowly stretched, making sure that she got a good look at my nude body.

"I think if my pubes were like yours," she said, studying me, "I might have kept them. You blondes are so lucky."

I'd had that said to me before. Most recently it had been George who'd commented on my colouring.

We were tired after the journey and went to bed soon

afterwards. I lay awake for a long time, my whole body aching for her. This wasn't the time to make a move, I knew. We would have two whole weeks together for me to choose the right moment. I lay with my finger touching my clitoris, but only when I was sure Debbie was fast asleep did I allow my fingers to start their magic work.

I fantasised about Debbie as I masturbated, imagining her long black hair cascading across my thighs while her head was between my legs, dreaming of my own mouth and lips and tongue moulding themselves into the softness of her hairless cunt. I tried not to make any noise, biting on my other hand to stifle my orgasmic cry when I came. Then I started all over again, rubbing myself to sleep.

But I never did get a chance with Debbie, because that was the only time we shared the room. Every other night I was alone, because she sneaked off somewhere. Presumably to fuck one of the guys in the team. Everyone was doing it, I discovered. The three models and the other girls in the crew were moving from bed to bed every night. George and I were the only ones excluded from this game, although I had several propositions. George, meanwhile, would be off on the prowl every evening after dinner.

Debbie and Sandra and Vanessa had difficulty understanding me.

"Don't you like fucking?" asked Debbie.

I shrugged.

"But everyone knows what these excursions are for. Sun and sea and sand and . . ." She pretended to frown. "What's the other thing?" Then she grinned. "Screwing's part of the job, how we unwind in the evenings. There must be someone here you fancy?"

She was concerned that I was missing out on the fun,

but there was no way that I could tell her who I did fancy. I'd heard the way they talked about George behind his back, even though it was obvious that they all liked him. So I remained silent.

"I couldn't get used to it at first," said Vanessa, "but I soon did. It's great. I don't want the same boring prick in my snatch every night. Variety is the spice of life. So taste life. Lick a different dick a day!"

They were all watching me, waiting for an answer. We were sitting nude on the beach, while George organised the unit for a shot of us silhouetted against the giant red setting sun.

"I'm a virgin," I said.

They all laughed as though it was the funniest thing they'd ever heard. I'd only told them because I knew they wouldn't believe me.

"What's that?"

"Never heard of one."

"I thought they were extinct."

"If you really want to know," I told them, "I'm a lesbian."

Their response was equally as amused and disbelieving.

"Come on," said Vanessa, "tell us the truth. Who did you have to fuck to get this job?"

"George," I said.

They glanced at one another, then without warning they all jumped me, grabbing hold of my arms and yanking me towards the edge of the sea, dragging me into the water, tripping me up and falling on top of me.

We collapsed into a giggling heap of bare boobs and buttocks, of thighs and twats, rolling about in two feet of ocean. I managed to seize hold of Debbie's ankle, pulling her through the water, spreading her legs and gazing into her forbidden pink cleft. Then Vanessa clutched hold of my arm, tugging me down with a massive splash.

I became aware of more splashing close by and I glanced around to see George plunging through the surf, the motor drive of his camera whirring as he photographed us.

"That's great, sweeties!" he yelled enthusiastically. "Keep it up. More. More. That's it. Get really into it. Great. More."

As he spoke, he beckoned to his assistant, who ran into the sea and handed him another camera. With hardly a pause he was shooting us again as we frolicked naked in the warm ocean. We dived upon each other, two of us ganging up to drag another under the surface. We were all scrabbling frantically for breath, but unable to stop laughing despite the water in our mouths, eyes, ears, cunts.

Over and over we rolled, kicking up the sand and water at each other, then flinging ourselves against the nearest nude body, tugging slender limbs, toppling backwards and then finally dropping exhaustedly in the shallows, panting, water dripping from our hair and down our breasts.

George was waist deep in the water, still fully dressed, still photographing, shouting at us not to stop.

Debbie glanced at me, I glanced at Vanessa, Vanessa glanced at Sandra, and without a word we launched ourselves at George. He saw us coming and tried to wade back towards the shore.

"The camera!" he shouted. "Mind the camera!" But even as he was warning us, he kept clicking the shutter.

Vanessa and I reached him first, hauling at his legs. As George fell, he kept one arm raised to hold his camera out of the sea, while his other hand held his glasses tight against his face so he didn't lose them.

Sandra seized the camera and hurled it towards Steve,

George's assistant, as George sank below the surface. Steve caught it then swiftly fled to the beach out of our reach.

George fought frantically and desperately as we began to strip him.

"Don't you dare!" he screamed, between gulps of water. "You'll never work again! Any of you! Get off me! Let go!"

Somehow he managed to twist away, leaving Debbie and Sandra holding his shirt. I hadn't been concentrating on George, instead gazing at my nubile companions. But the other three were taking this too seriously now, I realised. The photographer needed rescuing. So I pretended to stumble, and I managed to bring Debbie down beneath me, my hands caressing her hips as I feigned an attempt to save us both. Then George was free and heading back to the beach.

"Okay, sweeties," he said, both in anger and relief, as he reached the sand and turned to face us. "Fun's over, out you come." He used his fingers like windscreen wipers on his spectacle lenses. Looking beyond us, he noticed that the sun had begun to melt into the ocean. "Tomorrow is another day." He shrugged. "And another sunset."

The photos he'd taken would be no use for the calendar, but George also did magazine work. His more raunchy pictures found a ready market in the glossy men's publications. When he'd taken his first test shots of me, I'd been nude. George had wanted me to open my legs. But I wouldn't do that, not even for a camera.

Sandra followed George out, carrying his sodden shirt, and I admired the sway of her nude buttocks as she strode onto the beach. Vanessa had begun swimming parallel to the shore, her elegant arms and shapely legs propelling her in an easy crawl. And Debbie was floating on her back, only her face, the tips of her breasts and her hairless mound above the surface as she drifted a couple of yards away from me.

I watched her. I was sitting on the shallow sea bed, the water almost as high as my breasts, the flow of the current gently rocking me up and down. The ocean washed against my open labia, and I didn't even need to use my fingers to start bringing myself off. This was far better than any douching. The natural rhythm of the warm surging tide was in perfect harmony with my own internal pulses. I kicked myself gently upwards, thrusting out my arms to balance properly until I was floating on my back, edging towards Debbie, my legs wide apart.

We bumped into each other, and she cried out in surprise. I spun around, colliding with Debbie again and reaching out for her as if to save us both from going under when we rolled over together. As soon as I wrapped my arms around her naked body, feeling her breasts and hard nipples against my own, gripping one of her thighs tightly between my legs, I came.

Debbie held me against her, trying to steady us both, gazing curiously at me as I opened my mouth and gasped in ecstatic joy.

"Are you alright?" she asked.

I managed to nod my head.

"Good," she said. "For a moment I thought you were drowning."

She was almost correct: I'd been drowning in a flood of sensual gratification. It was obvious that she didn't suspect what had really happened. We found our feet, then made our way back to the shoreline together. There were four more days before we were due to fly home, away from this tropical paradise, and I knew that I'd never again be as sexually close to Debbie as I had been a minute earlier. But that no longer mattered, because I'd achieved my ambition – she had helped me reach fulfillment.

It had been an enjoyable experience, and it would continue in my mind as a happy memory. When I look back, my life is documented by such fondly recalled moments of pleasure. I try to forget all the rest, because who wants to remember the bad times?

And I remember the Caribbean trip as being one of the most important periods of my life, perhaps even the most important because . . .

SEVEN

The next evening we were again in position at the edge of the ocean as the sun went down, while George used up several rolls of film, yelling at us all the time to shift one way or the other, to bend over slightly, or to lean back so that the curves of our breasts showed up against the sun and the sky.

"Okay, sweeties," he announced, when the sun finally sank beneath the horizon, "let's call it a day."

His assistant and his assistant's assistant began to put away the equipment, while George came over towards us.

"We've only got two full days left," he said, as we began to dress. "And there are still two final shots."

"No problem," Debbie told him.

"Possibly not," George replied, "but we've got to make the most of the good weather. If there is any more good weather."

"What do you mean?" Vanessa wanted to know.

"There's a hurricane sweeping through the Caribbean," said George, "and there's a fair chance it could turn and head in our direction." He shrugged. "So I want to get as much done tomorrow as possible. We'll do that shot with Debbie and Sandra by the hotel pool tomorrow morning. In bed nice and early tonight please."

"Who with?" Sandra asked, smiling.

"With an early riser," George told her. Then he realised what he'd said. He thumped his forehead with the heel of his hand, while the three other girls giggled in amusement and made various ribald comments.

George watched them, shaking his head as if in disbelief, then he glanced wryly at me. "I'm glad you'll look as young and fresh as ever tomorrow, sweetie. Not like these old hags here. It's lucky all they ever have to do is lie around and have their photographs taken, because they'd never have the energy for anything else. They lie down at night, lie down during the day." He shook his head again, in mock sorrow. "I despair of this younger generation."

Debbie, Sandra and Vanessa pulled faces at him.

"You look better like that," George remarked. "Hold on, I'll get my camera."

We finished dressing and began heading to the vehicles parked on the single track road beyond the beach. But George put his hand on my arm, holding me back while the others went ahead.

"I've got to go to the other side of the island tonight," he said. "I want to scout out a location for the final shot. Do you want to come with me?"

It was more tempting than being stuck alone while the rest of the crew were busy fucking each other.

"Okay," I agreed. "But how can we see anything in the dark?"

"That's the idea," George said, and we began walking towards the road. "I want the final shot set at night, a single nude lit by moonlight. You'll be the model, although I don't want you to tell the others yet. It won't really be moonlight, but the lighting will seem like that. There's a full moon tomorrow, and you'll be on top of the island's highest point, with the sea in the distance. A full length frontal nude, but because of the light we'll have none of that taboo pubic hair. Your long blonde hair will be the focus of the shot. I can see it perfectly in my mind, and I want to see if the location will work for tomorrow."

"Sounds wonderful," I said, and it did. But I wondered whether George would have given me the final picture if I hadn't agreed to go with him tonight. It depended which had the most priority: a blonde or the lack of pubic hair. I was the only blonde of the four models, but Debbie would be the easiest to shoot if he didn't want any cunt hairs – not that he'd want her slit visible either.

"That's settled, sweetie," he said. "We'll go off now, have a meal on the way, then see what this place is like at midnight. We'll be back late, but you won't have to get up early tomorrow."

"Can't we go back to the hotel so I can change?"

"You look fine. We don't want to waste time."

I didn't think I looked fine. All I was wearing was a pair of old jeans, a woollen sweater and a pair of sandals. I didn't even have any underwear. Despite the heat of the day, it soon became cold when the sun was down. I needed some other clothes if we would be out late; and if we were going to a restaurant, I'd have preferred to have a better outfit. But George was the boss, so I merely shrugged in resignation.

He commandeered one of the cars, told the rest of the crew where we were going – not that anyone particularly cared – and we drove off one way while the other vehicles headed in the opposite direction. There was no need for a map, because the island was so small that there were very few proper roads. The one we were on led away from the capital and straight through the hills towards the other side of the isle.

The road became worse the further we went, and George had to slow down because of all the holes and cracks in the surface. It was clear that we were leaving the tourist area, and we hardly saw any other cars. After a while we came across a small hotel, and we parked outside then went in for a meal.

We had a couple of drinks first, two bottles of wine while we ate, and a couple more drinks afterwards.

"It was only three weeks ago that you took me for that first meal," I said as we sat at a table in the bar. We'd been on bar stools before the meal, but by silent agreement we'd now chosen less precarious seating. Having drunk so much, it wouldn't have been safe to risk high stools.

"Is that all, sweetie?" said George. "It seems more like twenty-one days to me." He grinned. "But this was a much better meal at a tenth of the price, right?"

I nodded in agreement.

"Are you enjoying yourself?" George asked. This was about the only time he and I had been alone together since we'd arrived in the Caribbean.

"Very much," I told him, truthfully.

"You get on well with the other girls?"

"Yes, of course. They're fun and I've learned a lot from them."

"They're a randy trio," said George. "Which is why they go on these trips so often. But I've noticed that you haven't been . . . er . . . indulging in similar carnal activities. That's something you haven't learned from them."

Everyone else in the team knew about my lack of sexual activity. Amongst so few, the story had soon spread. In their eyes I was an ice cold frigid blonde.

I shook my head. "I have to be in love," I sighed, but I was unable suppress a smile.

"And Debbie's the one, isn't she?" said George.

I stared at him, startled. There was no point denying it. "Is it that obvious?" I asked.

"Probably only to me. I'm sure Debbie is unaware of your feelings for her."

I said nothing, because there was nothing to be said.

"I could stay here all night," George said, staring into his empty glass. "But there's work to be done. Shall we carry on our journey?"

"Is that wise? You've had a lot to drink."

"But not enough. I'll buy a bottle of rum to take with us. Don't worry. Never drink and drive, I always say. That way you never spill any!" He laughed, then called over the barman. "Don't worry, sweetie. There aren't any other cars on the road, so we'll be okay."

A few minutes later we were on our way back to the car. I noticed it was more windy than it had been a couple of hours ago, and the sky was overcast. The moon and stars could no longer been seen through the dark clouds. It would have been futile to point this out to George, because he'd have thought I was trying to evade the midnight mountaineering which he'd planned.

We climbed into the car and resumed our expedition, and I tried not to consider that I could have been in my comfortable hotel room with a good paperback. But that was what I'd been doing every night since we'd arrived, so at least this made a change. George was driving more cautiously now, because he knew he had to. But before long he asked me to open the bottle of rum, and he swigged it as he drove.

The car moved slowly through the darkness, bouncing across the rough road surface and buffeted by the winds. It began to rain, a few heavy drops suddenly splattering against the windscreen. After a few attempts on the horn and indicators, George managed to find the wipers; but by then the rain had stopped as quickly as it had begun.

"Soon be there," he assured me.

"Soon be there," he repeated half an hour later, and by that time I was helping him with the rum. The first gulp burned my throat with its fierce rawness, but after that I got used to it.

Then to my surprise, George suddenly announced, "Here we are."

The car stopped, and it was so dark outside that we could have been almost anywhere. Assuming this was the place George had been heading for, I admired the way he'd managed to bring us here. I felt quite light-headed, and from the amount he'd consumed George must have been at least as drunk as I was.

He climbed out of the driver's seat, and I also left the car. I realised that we were quite high, because in the distance I could make out the sea. It was brighter than the land in between, reflecting what little light there was. The wind was even stronger now.

"Up there," said George.

My gaze followed his pointing finger, and I saw a dark shadow looming up in the sky ahead of us. As my eyes became accustomed to the gloom, I recognised it as a soaring peak of rock thrusting up into the black sky.

"Come on." George beckoned to me, then started walking. He was carrying one camera slung around his neck; he had his gadget bag hung over his shoulder; and he carried the bottle of rum.

I hurried to catch up with him, staring up at the bleak precipice which confronted us. Despite being drunk, I knew that this was crazy. We couldn't possibly get up there, not in the dark. It would be bad enough in the daylight. And sober.

But as we came closer, I realised that the light was deceptive. The pinnacle of rock was nearer than I'd thought, and not so daunting and impossible as it seemed at a distance. There was even a path which led towards it, and then a flight of concrete steps. Everything had been made easier for the tourists, for which I was grateful, because I tripped and stumbled even on the footpath.

We made our way towards the summit, where the wind was blowing even more.

"Clothes off, sweetie," said George, and I obeyed.

I unzipped my jeans and let them fall, stepping out of my sandals as well as the denims, then I pulled my sweater off and folded it on top of my other garment. Naked, I shivered in the sharp breeze.

At that moment a blazing streak of lightning abruptly split the darkness, and the sky became as bright as day. A few seconds later came the rumble of distant thunder.

George was standing opposite, watching me through his camera viewfinder. It seemed he hadn't been aware of the lightning.

"I want the sea beyond you," he said. "There. Yes. The moon will be behind you tomorrow night, and we'll light you from that angle. I want to take a few preliminary shots now."

I heard the shutter click. George must have been using a very fast film, because there was no flash. That came a few moments later, as a second streak of lightning illuminated the peak. The interval until the thunder was less this time; the storm was rapidly approaching. It began to rain, only a few heavy drops at first, which fell onto my nude body.

The rain was warm, and I turned my face up towards the sky, letting the drops fall into my open mouth. My hair was blowing in the wind, my skin goose-pimpled from the chill, my nipples hard. Then the rain suddenly became a torrent, and in moments I was as wet as I'd have been under a shower. The lightning flashed; the thunder roared.

I wiped my hand across my dripping face; I could hardly see George through the tropical deluge. This was crazy, I thought, and I bent down for my clothes.

"No!" he shouted. He moved closer, going down on one knee and aiming the camera up at me. "Stay there, sweetie. Tilt your head back. Raise your arms to the sky. Turn. Again. Back. Towards me. This is great! Spread your arms. Spread your legs. Point to the sky. Now with the other arm. Lean back. Turn. More. More. Yes! Both arms out. Toss your head. Run your fingers through your hair. Look angry. Serious. Happy. Sad. Worried. Frightened. Great! Put your hands on your tits. Stroke them. Now to your crotch. No! Just one hand. The other to the sky. Turn around. Right around. Keep going. Move your arms. Now hang your head in despair. Now both arms high. Head raised. Yes. Great! Yes. Yes. Yes!"

I did as I was told, not thinking, letting George direct me as though I was a puppet on a string. All the time his camera was clicking away, while in the background the lightning flashed across the sky and the thunder rumbled menacingly. I was soaked through, and so was George.

At last he rose to his feet, and I realised that he must have been out of film. He gazed at me as he brushed his fingers through his hair, then tried to dry his glasses with his wet sleeve. He shook his head, lifted the bottle of rum to his mouth and took a deep swig. He wiped the back of his hand across his lips. And at last he smiled.

"That was," he said, slowly, "unbelievable."

Although neither of us knew it then, George had already taken one of the final shots for the calendar, the picture for which it became most famous. It showed me like some primitive tribal priestess, naked against the savage fury of the storm, arms outstretched, seeming to conjure jagged lightning from my fingertips, while the angry wind blew my wet mane of blonde hair behind me. Although I was clearly nude, the sky cast an incandescent aura which illuminated only the curve of my breasts and thighs and the flatness of my stomach; my cunt was modestly shadowed, nature acting as the censor to make the photograph suitable for the drinks company's purpose. Their only complaint was that the prehistoric sorceress wasn't holding a bottle of their product in one hand, but even they accepted this would have looked ridiculous.

I picked up my clothes, slipped on my sandals. George took my hand as we raced down the steep hill towards the car. We jumped inside and slammed the doors, panting for breath but laughing in drunken euphoria.

George was watching me. I was still naked.

"Nude girls and cars," he said, more to himself than to me. "We haven't used that image. But I suppose they aren't selling oil or tyres." He held his camera up, staring at me through the viewfinder. "No more film," he muttered. Then he reached for the rum again, and he passed it to me.

I gulped from the bottle. "Thanks."

The rain pelted noisily against the roof and windows of the car, while the wind rocked the vehicle from side to side.

"I don't know what's the best thing to do," George said, after a couple of mouthfuls. "Whether I should take my wet clothes off or you should put your wet clothes on."

I shivered. "Put the heater on," I suggested.

He slid the key into the ignition, then turned it. He twisted the key back, turned it again.

"Ohhhhhh . . . shit!"

"What?"

"The car won't start," he said, frantically twisting the key to the left and right.

"Why not?"

"I'm a photographer, sweetie," he explained, patiently, "not a mechanic. How should I know why it won't start?"

I knew nothing about cars; I couldn't even drive. All I knew was that I felt cold, I was trembling, and my clothes were soaking wet.

"We'll die of pneumonia if we stay here," I said. "Can't we push the car?"

"All the way back?"

"Push start it." I said, angrily. "You know what I mean."

"This is an automatic, sweetie. We can't push start it."

"I thought you weren't a mechanic."

"That's right. But I did once try to push an automatic. When I was younger and stupider. Which is why I know it's impossible."

"So what do we do?"

"Good question," said George. "Very good question. If you've got any ideas, let me know." He raised the bottle to his lips again.

I twisted my hair, bunching it in my fists and squeezing out as much water as I could. As I turned my head, I thought I saw a light further down the road, then the swirling rain obscured it from my vision. A few seconds later, the light flickered through the darkness again.

"There's a light down there," I said, pointing. "It must be a car coming up here." I began pulling on my sodden clothes.

George peered out through the torrential rain. "I see it," he confirmed. After a minute he added, "It's not coming any closer. They must have stopped." He glanced at me. "Shall we go down to them? It might be the only chance we'll get. Otherwise we'll be stuck here all night."

I nodded in agreement. Anything was better than staying in the car, and neither of us could have become any wetter. So we left the vehicle, George with his camera bag, and headed down the road in the direction of the light. We fought our way through the sheets of rain and strong gusts of wind, until the water poured off us in bucketfuls.

It wasn't a car that I'd seen, it was a house. There was another road which forked off the route which led to the summit, and the building was tucked away on the side of the hill, out of sight of the junction. It wasn't very big, but it was solidly constructed and looked expensive.

We pushed through one of the double wrought iron gates at the end of the drive and hurried towards the front door. The light we'd seen came from a lamp in the porch. Apart from that, everything was dark.

George knocked on the door, and a minute later he knocked again, louder and longer. A light came on inside, and a few seconds later the front door opened slightly.

"Hello," said George. "Sorry to disturb you so late, but our car has broken down. Can we use your telephone to call up a garage?"

The door opened wider, and a middle-aged man wearing

a dressing gown stared at us in amazement. Then he shook his head. "A garage? Where the hell do you think this is? There aren't any garages around here." He spoke perfect English, but there was a strong foreign accent to his voice.

"What about a taxi?" asked George.

The man laughed, shaking his head again. He stepped back. "You'd better come in," he said, which was what we did. "Celine!" he called. "Have you got a couple of towels for our visitors?"

A plump woman of about forty appeared from a doorway along the hall, then vanished again. When she reappeared, she was carrying two bath towels.

"You best come through here," she told me, and I recognised her accent as French. She gave George and me one of the towels each.

"Thanks," I said, and I followed her through into the front room, towelling my hair as I did so. I could hear George still questioning the man behind us.

"If there isn't a taxi, can I use your phone? I must contact my colleagues."

"The phone isn't working."

"Lines down because of the hurricane?" George asked.

"Hurricane?" repeated the man, and he laughed briefly. "What hurricane? This is nothing. You just wait and see what it's like when there really is a hurricane!"

"Then why isn't the phone working?"

"I don't know. This isn't the centre of Paris, my friend. We can't expect the same kind of facilities."

The two men came into the front room. I had the towel wrapped tight around me, to keep myself from shivering. The Frenchman stared at me.

"A glass of cognac, I think," he remarked. "That is what you two need." He walked to an intricately carved wooden cabinet in the corner and produced a bottle of brandy. He poured two glasses, hesitated, then tipped more brandy into another two of the huge glasses which were almost large enough to keep goldfish in. All four of us sipped at our drinks, and I could feel the strong liquor warming my throat, the heat radiating through my body.

After we'd both said thanks, George wanted to know, "But if there isn't a telephone, what can we do?"

"You must stay here," the woman told him. "We have spare bedroom. Everything prepared, because my son and his wife arrive tomorrow afternoon."

"Correct," agreed her husband. "And in the morning perhaps the phone will be working and the rain have stopped. You can obtain mechanical assistance. Or if you are in a hurry, then we can summon a taxi from the capital."

"But . . ." George began, then he shrugged, realising that there was no way of getting the car started or returning to our hotel tonight. "This is very kind of you, but we can't possibly accept your offer."

I stared at him in disbelief. What did he mean?

"That is up to you, my friend," the man said. "If you wish to walk back to your car in the rain and remain there all night, then of course you may." He looked at me. "And you, young lady?"

"I'd like to stay here," I told him. "Thank you."

I noticed George glance at me, and suddenly I realised what the problem was: that we'd have to share the same bedroom. Or at least George saw it as a problem, although I couldn't understand why.

"We'd both like to stay," I continued, taking the initiative. "George is worried about the car, that's all." I introduced myself and George.

"Pleased to meet you both," said the man, shaking George's hand, then taking my own and raising it to his lips in a gentle kiss. "My name is Louis, and this is Celine, my wife."

"Is enough talk, Louis," said the woman. "You not see poor girl is exhausted? All she want is get out of wet clothes and go to bed. We can talk in morning."

"You go ahead, sweetie," said George. "Get some rest. I'll sleep on the sofa here so I won't disturb you."

Louis watched him, then gazed at me before glancing back to George. As I left the room I heard him say, "Don't worry, my friend. It's a very big bed, and the walls are thick." He laughed again, and then came the sound of him slapping George's back. I wished I could have seen George's expression.

"Bathroom through there," said Celine, as she led me along the hall. She nodded to a door opposite the one she opened. She leaned inside and switched on the bedroom light. "Is anything you need?"

I shook my head. "No thanks," I told her. "This is very kind of you."

She smiled and patted my arm. "Leave wet clothes outside door, and I dry them. I see you tomorrow. Good night."

"Good night," I echoed. I stepped into the bedroom and pushed the door shut.

The room was sparsely furnished, but all I was interested in was the bed. There was nothing else I wanted except to sleep. I was so tired that I could have slept almost anywhere.

But the double bed, with its deep pillows, was my idea of heaven right at that moment.

I shed my shoes and peeled off my wet clothes, putting them out of the door as Celine had asked. Drying myself as best I could, I slid naked between the sheets and sat up while I gave my damp hair a last towelling. I wasn't thinking of George. Where he slept was his problem.

But as I yawned and let the towel drop to the floor, the door opened and George entered the room. He shut the door and leaned against it, staring at me. I fell back against the soft pillows, tugging up the covers under my chin.

"You're having that side of the bed?" George asked.

"Ye -," I yawned again "—ah. Are you having the other side?"

"If that's okay by you, sweetie."

Even if it had bothered me, I was too tired to care. "Don't look so worried, George. We're only sleeping together," I joked.

He would have to strip off completely, because his clothes were as soaked as mine. It was this which seemed to be making him so nervous. First he took off his shoes and socks, then his jacket and shirt. He used the towel to dry his torso and hair. But even before he removed his slacks, he switched off the light.

"George!" I said, with mock severity. "How many times have you seen me naked? Aren't you even going to let me have a peep at your prick?"

"No," he said.

Despite my tiredness, I quickly pushed back the covers and crept out of bed, silently making my way towards the light switch. I had no particular wish to see George's cock, but I wasn't going to let him get away with this. He treated our nudity so casually, but he was embarrassed by the prospect of being seen without his clothes. It wasn't even as though I wanted to take his photograph.

I reached the switch and flicked it on, but I wasn't fast enough. George was almost in bed, and he managed to pull the covers across his vital zone.

He grinned at me. "Too late, sweetie."

I shook my head, pointing to his clothes on the floor. "If you don't put your things out, Celine won't be able to dry them."

"Put them out for me, will you?"

"Say 'please'," I told him.

"Please."

"No."

"Okay." George reached for the towel on the chair next to him, wrapped it around his waist, climbed out of bed, picked up his clothes, put them outside of the door, then returned to bed, replacing the towel on the chair, then removing his glasses.

I grabbed the towel and threw it into the far corner. "You wait till tomorrow morning," I told him, and I switched the light off and climbed into bed. We lay at opposite ends, as far away from each other as possible. "Good night."

"Good night," said George.

I was asleep within seconds.

That night I dreamed, dreamed a long languid erotic fantasy.

I was naked, wandering alone through the wilderness of Arctic glaciers, cold and trembling. Everywhere was so silent and still, and I tried to run to keep warm. But my feet wouldn't react properly, and so I moved in slow motion through the freezing wasteland. My breath condensed in white clouds in front of my face, and my nipples stood defensively erect against the unbearable cold. I had to find some warmth or else I wouldn't survive.

In the distance I saw something which seemed out of place, and as I came closer I realised that it was an igloo. A dome-shaped house of ice, its entrance a sharp vertical gash through the curve of the wall. Without hesitating, I ducked my head and went inside. And there at eye level, the first thing I saw, was a shaven cunt.

I stood upright inside the igloo, and Debbie was waiting for me, as nude as I was. She opened her arms in welcome, and I moved closer to her. We embraced, holding each other tight, our bodies pressed close against each other. Breasts against breasts, pubis against pubis, thighs against thighs. Gradually we sank down, falling onto the animal furs which lined the floor, our hands exploring each other's bodies. We hadn't yet kissed, but there was no haste; we had all the time in the world.

I felt the warmth of Debbie's body, caressing her smooth supple curves with my palms. She was above me, warming me with her heat, and I clutched her buttocks to hold her close. Her hands stroked my breasts, and then she lowered her head to my left breast, her mouth circling the nipple, sucking and teasing it with her pursed lips, the tip of her tongue delicately licking my areola. Then she moved to my other breast, her lips and tongue concentrating on the nipple but stimulating my whole body.

She raised her head, and at last we kissed. My lips parted, and Debbie's mouth was against mine, her tongue probing inside and finding my own tongue. Our lips rubbed fiercely together, tongues thrusting and counter-thrusting.

One of her hands slid down and found my cunt; a finger slipped between my moist labia. It felt so good to have her delicately stroking my clitoris. I reached for her twat, my right hand leaving her buttocks and sliding around her waist, slipping down her stomach and through her soft pubic hairs, then—

—then I began to wake up, because I realised that Debbie didn't have pubic hairs.

And I discovered this was no dream when my hand touched the rigid shape of a warm penis as it gently eased its way inside me . . .

I came instantly awake, my eyes opening. In the moonlight filtering through the window I saw George, his mouth locked against mine, his weight supported on his elbows as he slipped his cock into me. Our eyes met, he lifted his face away from mine and he smiled as his knob slid all the way in.

I pulled my mouth free from his, gasping for breath, but otherwise unable to move. George did the moving, his hips rocking up as he drew his tool back, back, then down as he drove it back in, in.

I was being fucked!

This was what it was like to have a cock inside me, a man making love to me.

It was unbelievable.

I'd never felt or experienced anything like it. The sensation was amazing. To feel the flesh of George's knob sliding over my clit, rubbing against the lips of my vulva, stroking the walls of my cunt, was mind shattering. It was a total revelation and my whole being glowed with erotic awareness. My own fingers, even Carole's tongue, had never been half so fantastic.

Instinctively I began to move my hips, pushing against George, then moving with him. My arms went around his back, tugging his lean body even closer against my breasts, drawing him down so that we could kiss again. I tasted his tongue, felt the stubble around his lips, enjoyed his maleness plunging into me – and I wondered why I'd wasted so much of my life in avoiding the ultimate hedonistic encounter.

We were as one, working in total harmony, our bodies made for each other. My softness was complemented by his ruggedness. We fitted together like some precision built machine, my eager cunt the perfect fit for his thrusting cock, because that was what nature had designed them for.

I felt a trembling deep within, the first signal of an impending orgasm which promised so much. I kissed George with more passion, urging him further into me, deeper and deeper, harder and harder. Every inch of my flesh was aglow with desire; every sense was heightened; every muscle throbbed with sexual potential.

Above me I heard George breathing faster and faster, and I knew that he must be about to come. But I didn't want that. Not yet. I wasn't ready. I didn't want to be left stranded high and dry.

I reached for his hips, trying to hold him back. But he was too powerful and simply kept on pumping into me, his prick stimulating every sensitive nerve ending in my vagina, bringing me to my zenith – although not quickly enough.

Then with one final deep drive, George tensed and became completely rigid. A moment later, he sighed with absolute satisfaction as he climaxed.

I felt his seed spurt into me, swirling hotly against my inner flesh, and the unique sensation spurred on my own inner contractions. I cried out in helpless ecstasy, my fingers clawing at George's back, my entire body convulsing as it shuddered with overwhelming pleasure.

And I came and came and came and came.

EIGHT

I never did get to see George's cock, because when I woke up the next morning he was already dressed and sitting on the edge of the bed. I lay without moving, staring at him.

George smiled wryly, then shrugged.

"Why don't you come back to bed?" I suggested. "I might enjoy it more if I was awake from the beginning."

"What are you talking about?" he asked.

"You know what I'm talking about. The way you fucked me last night."

George put his hand on his chest. "Me?" he asked, in astonishment. "You must have been dreaming, sweetie. I don't fuck girls."

I raised the bed clothes, staring down at my naked body, pretending to check that I really was female.

"I didn't have my glasses on last night," said George. He was grinning broadly by now. "And whatever you say," he added, "I'll deny it."

"I won't say anything if you get back in here," I told him.

He shook his head. "I'm properly awake now, too," he pointed out. "I mean it, sweetie, don't say anything. It won't do my reputation my good."

"I don't understand this," I said, sitting up and letting the covers fall away from my breasts.

"What is there to understand? You were cold last night, and I warmed you up. That's all. Any complaints?"

There was more to it than George implied. He hadn't

fucked me just for my benefit. But I shook my head. "No, no complaints," I told him. And there weren't.

"That's what I like to hear," he said. "Come on, up you get. Our hosts have got breakfast ready. The phone's working, and we have to get back to work. Can't leave that lazy lot in the hotel doing nothing."

"You've done it before," I said.

"What?"

"Fucked girls. You aren't gay."

"I am, sweetie. I can go either way, but I prefer guys. You've tried both, so which do you prefer?"

"Let's do it again and I'll tell you."

George laughed, leaning forward to kiss my forehead. I grabbed hold of him, trying to force his lips against mine, but he slipped away and stood up.

I'd forgotten how much I needed someone else, another body to hold against me, someone to love. Male or female, either would do – although with what I knew now I had to admit there was no substitute for a good stiff prick. Which reminded me . . .

"George," I asked, "will you do me a favour?"

"For you, sweetie, anything. What is it?"

"I'd like to see your penis."

"What!" he said, as though it was the most outrageous thing he'd ever heard in his life. He shook his head. "Anything but that. I'm the photographer, you're the model, remember? You take your clothes off, not me. What do you think I am, some kind of pervert?" He laughed, then opened the door and was gone.

Which is how I lost my virginity to a homosexual while I was half-asleep. And I never did get to see those first few inches of flesh which changed the course of my life. George had done a lot for me already, but I can never thank him enough for what he did that night.

George wasn't strictly gay; he was prepared to accept whatever was available. After thinking that I was a lesbian, it was a revelation to learn that there was far more to life than just girls – or really only one of them. Because although I'd fantasised about other women such as Sue and Debbie, Carole was the only girl I'd ever been intimate with. Girl? She was the only person I'd been to bed with until my first man had come along, in the unlikely character of George.

He was bisexual, although his inclination was towards partners of his own sex. And now I could see how that might be the best solution. Why cut yourself off from half of the human race when it was possible to fuck all of them? If I restricted myself to one gender, either male or female, that meant I'd miss out on half of my sexual potential.

As I said, I learned a lot from George. He'd already changed my life by helping me escape from the drudgery of office work, and now he had expanded my orgasmic horizons as well.

After Celine and Louis gave us breakfast and we thanked them, we were picked up by the vehicle which the car hire agency had sent as replacement, and we returned to the capital. Immediately he was back, George started working again, taking up a position on the diving board above the swimming pool for a shot of Sandra and Debbie floating prone and naked on inflatable mattresses, sipping at their drinks through straws.

I hardly bothered looking at the girls, not even at Debbie. Why should I torture myself in yearning for the impossible when I'd sampled other less elusive delights?

We only had two more nights in the Caribbean, but I was

determined to make the most of them. I knew it was hopeless thinking of George again, but he wasn't the only available male in the crew. There were his two assistants and the two lighting men, plus the four other guys who were in the team – the pair who did the most menial tasks, plus the other two who handled the administration and finance. This didn't include all the other men in the hotel, the guests and staff. While beyond the hotel there were even more potential partners . . .

As George directed the shot, I studied the possibilities. The other eight men were clustered around the pool, while Debbie and Sandra drifted across the surface. That offered me several intriguing permutations. Old or young? Tall or short? Fat or thin? Their occupations didn't matter, because I only wanted them for one reason.

I could have asked Vanessa for her recommendations, because she must have tried them all. But I had to find out for myself, use my own judgement. The big question was: where should I start?

Even the guys who weren't directly involved with the photo sessions almost always hung around the girls, watching. The novelty of the models' naked bodies hadn't worn off. I didn't blame the men at all, because I liked to look myself. There was something very aesthetically pleasing about a female nude. I began wondering about male nudes. I hadn't seen George or his equipment. In fact, the only man I'd ever seen totally unclad had been that stripper a couple of months ago. It seemed much further in my past than that, because so much had happened since.

The two guys who handled the business side of the unit were the only ones not needed at the poolside. They were called Tom and Roger, and they'd both tried propositioning me soon after we arrived in the Caribbean. When I'd ignored them, they'd gone in search of more willing prey.

Now it was their turn to ignore me. We'd taken over the whole pool for the morning, and I stood in the tunnel which led to the changing rooms, out of sight of everyone except Tom and Roger. They were standing together by the water's edge, talking. I hadn't returned to my room and was still wearing the same jeans and jumper, so I chose the simplest way of attracting their attention: I took off my clothes and slung them over one shoulder. It was Roger who noticed me first. He was about five yards away from me, and our eyes met. Then I turned and slowly walked back along the tunnel. Without having to look around, I sensed he was following me.

I went into the male changing room. It was lined with benches, a row of cubicles in the centre. I walked around to the far side of the room, away from the door, and took a huge towel from a peg to spread on the ground. Folding my jeans into a pillow, I lay down on the floor and waited for Roger.

He found me, and without a word he reached for his zip. Roger was an average sort of guy, with no distinguishing features. And when I'd had more experience of these things, I realised that even his cock had been quite average. It was already horizontal as he dropped his pants, stiffening more and rising higher as I watched.

He knelt down between my legs, his hands stroking my inner thighs and forcing them wider apart. He didn't look at my face, simply stared at my cunt. That was okay, because neither was I interested in his face – only the length of firm flesh which jutted from between his legs. His right hand came down on my crotch, palm rotating against my pubis, thumb pressing against my moist cleft, while his left hand reached for my right breast, stroking it and lightly pinching the nipple between his fingers.

This must have been Roger's idea of foreplay, because after about ten seconds and without further preliminary, he let go and moved further back so he could lie down on top of me. His left hand came down on the ground by my head, while his right guided his shaft towards the open lips of my cunt. I was already wet, and his knob slid smoothly inside. Without a pause he began thrusting his buttocks, fast and furious. His right hand went to my left boob, fondling it, while his fingertips circled around and around the nipple.

I closed my eyes, and my own hips began jerking up and down to meet his. He was giving me exactly what I wanted, several virile inches of male flesh gliding within my twat, transmitting the delicious tremors to every atom of my body. This was sex, pure sex, nothing but basic fucking, without such distracting formalities as kissing or affection. And I adored it.

Suddenly his come flooded into my cunt, and Roger sank down on top of me and became still, except for his hands which gently stroked my face as his heartbeat slowed and his breathing returned to normal.

I hadn't climaxed, and I tried to rub myself against his cock, but he withdrew. I opened my eyes in disappointment as he stood up, and I realised for the first time that we weren't alone. Tom was leaning against the row of cubicles, watching.

I stared up at Roger, at his prick which was wilting and shrinking, no longer any use for my needs. Then I put him out of my mind and instead gazed at Tom, short chubby Tom. He read the message, stepping forwards and undoing his pants. His fat cock sprang free, primed for action, and moments later he was down on the ground with me.

It was Roger's turn to watch, but I didn't care. All I wanted was Tom and his penis. He lay next to me, tugging me over onto my side by him, his arms stroking my body, his tongue and lips everywhere. But I didn't want that, what I needed was him deep within me. I reached for his prick, grabbing hold of it, scarcely realising that this was the first one I'd held – my brief touch of George's tool hardly counted. I rolled onto my back again, and Tom was on top of me, while I rubbed his glans against my clitoris.

He refused to be rushed. His mouth found my left nipple, sucking it tenderly before switching his attention to my right tit. His hands stroked my shoulders, my rib cage, my stomach, my hips, my thighs.

I panted, my whole body itching to feel his cock penetrating me. But still Tom held back, noisily nuzzling the lobe of my left ear, then kissing my neck and throat. My hand slid down the length of his tool, finding the hairy roundness of his testicles, examining them with my fingertips. Then I took a firmer grip on his shaft, my hand returning towards the glans, feeling the outer skin slide in my grip as I jerked his prick against my vaginal lips.

"Now," I begged. "I want it now. Give it to me."

"What?" Tom teased. "What do you want?"

"I want your cock."

"My cock? What for?"

"I want it in me," I breathed.

"Why?"

"I want you to fuck me."

"You want me to fuck you?"

"Yes!"

"Say it again," he ordered.

"I want you to fuck me. Fuck me. Fuck me!"

"And what do I get out of it?" Tom asked.

"My cunt!" I was almost shouting now.

"Your cunt?" said Tom.

His fingertips brushed between my labia, and I gasped with delight at this sudden extra contact. But then Tom retreated, caressing my thighs instead.

"I can have it now, can I?" he continued. "What if I don't want it? There's plenty of other cunt. You wouldn't let me have it last week, so why should I take it now? What's your cunt got that the others haven't?"

I threw one arm back, barely able to answer as I writhed on the floor, my other hand still stroking the swollen head of his phallus against my twat. "Cunt," I sighed, "so . . . hot . . . so . . . tight . . . so . . . juicy . . ."

"That right, Roger?" Tom wanted to know. His tongue traced a line beneath my breasts as he turned his head slightly to look at the other man, who was watching with amusement.

"I've fucked worse," Roger commented, speaking for the first time since he'd entered the changing room.

"Shall I give it to her?" Tom asked.

"Why not?" said Roger.

"Shall I?" Tom asked me.

"Yes," I pleaded. "Yes, yes, yes!"

As Tom slowly slid his prick into me, my entire being trembled, and I was instantly transported to the same moment of imminent satisfaction I'd reached when Roger has so abruptly climaxed.

Frantically, I began rocking my hips to and fro, stroking myself against the length of hard cock which had impaled me. With agonising slowness, Tom pulled back until his glans almost came free, then he shoved forward again, then nearly out, back in again, then out. For each seemingly endless cycle, I must have rubbed myself a dozen times against him.

My hands clutched the stiffness of his manhood, feeling the flesh as it buried itself deep into my throbbing twat, my fingers caressing the lips of my vulva and my pulsing clitoris.

I gasped for breath, and then without warning I peaked, the thunderous orgasmic eruptions causing me to scream uncontrollably until my lungs were empty.

Just as I was recovering, Tom's prick began to spout, his jet of spunk igniting another fiery climax within. And I moaned with pleasure as the inferno consumed me.

Slowly recovering, I stared up at Tom: his teeth bared, his eyes firmly shut, his nostrils flared. After a few seconds his eyes opened, and he saw me watching him. He kissed the tip of my nose.

"Why did you take so long before deciding to join the party?" he asked, as he pulled free and stood up.

"I'm a slow starter," I told him.

"But when you start up," he said, "you really go."

I was looking at his cock. It was pinker now, because of its exertions, and damp from my cunt juice. A drop of semen leaked from the end of its swollen purple head, and it hung down like a glowing stalactite before finally falling free and dripping to the ground. Tom's dick was gradually becoming detumescent.

Roger's prick was hardly in any more serviceable condition, although I wondered if he intended to return and carry on where he'd left off. I watched him expectantly, hoping. But now that Tom was no longer screwing me, Roger seemed to lose interest as well.

They hauled their pants up from around their ankles; they hadn't even bothered undressing.

"See you later," said Tom.

"Yeah," agreed Roger. Then they walked out of the changing room and left me lying on the floor.

I sighed contentedly. After a while, I stretched and stood up. As I regained my feet, I felt something warm and wet trickle from my cunt and run onto my thighs. Roger's and Tom's intermingled spunk, creamy and sticky. I stepped into my jeans, pulling them up tight, rubbing the semen all over my legs and across my pubic hairs. Then I put on my sandals and sweater, left the towel where it lay, and headed back towards the pool.

Everything was exactly as it had been. Debbie and Sandra still floated aimlessly on the water, while George balanced on the end of the diving board behind his tripod, shouting out instructions to the crew. Tom and Roger were chatting as before, and they didn't even turn their heads to look at me. Not that I was looking at them, either: my attention was focused on the other six men in the unit. We had forty-eight hours before leaving the Caribbean. That was one of them every six hours, which ought to be no problem.

I went for a shower and to wash my hair, and the others were still working when I returned. In my white shorts and with sleeveless blouse unbuttoned and knotted at the waist, I no longer felt so over-dressed. Going to the beach, I found Vanessa asleep under a huge parasol near the edge of the sparkling sea, wearing only the lower half of a tiny bikini. I woke her, she pulled on the man's shirt she wore as a top and we went to the hotel bar for a lunch of sea food and alcohol.

The picture of Debbie and Sandra in the pool was the penultimate shot, the last scheduled one being that night on top of the hill George and I had already visited. If everything went well, our last full day would be a free day. That was assuming the final two sessions produced suitable photographs. George's first and second assistants would develop and print the shots, but if anything went wrong we'd have to work on the final day. I hoped nothing would, because I'd planned a busy enough schedule already.

Before we drove to the other side of the island, most of us had the afternoon free to make up for the extra hours we'd be working when it was dark. The other girls did exactly what they'd been doing for the rest of the fortnight when they weren't fucking, they lazed around on the beach. I went up to the hotel room which was being used as the photographic darkroom.

The first assistant was inside, and he opened the door when I knocked. I'd been there a few times before, because I was interested in finding out what the photographs of me were like. Perhaps it was because I was vain, or maybe it was simply that I wasn't used to being photographed. In time the novelty might wear off, as it had done for the other three.

"Hello, Steve," I said.

"Hi," he greeted me. "What can I do for you?" He looked me up and down, clearly signalling what he'd like to do for me.

"A couple of things," I replied. "Have you developed those test pictures George took last night?"

Steve shook his head. "Not yet."

"Okay. In that case, why don't we fuck?"

He stared at me blankly, as though he didn't understand what the word meant. Steve was the oldest man in the team, in his forties, solidly built, with a pushed-in face which made him look as though he'd walked into a wall. He blinked his heavy-lidded eyes.

"You can spare a few minutes, can't you?" I asked. I reached for the "Do Not Disturb" sign, hung it on the outside door handle, then pushed the door shut.

Steve still hadn't moved, and now he frowned uncertainly. To convince him, I unknotted the front of my blouse and slipped it off my shoulders, then pushed down my shorts. Steve had seen me naked before, but not when we'd been alone together.

"Is this some kind of joke?" he asked.

I didn't answer. "Is something wrong with me, Steve? I know you've fucked all the other girls, so isn't it about time you gave me some of your cock?" I moved closer to him, reaching for his zip.

But he pushed my hand away. "I can do that," he said.

There was a single bed against the far wall, but it was covered with negatives and contact prints. Steve walked across to the bed, carefully picking up all the things and setting them neatly on the floor. Only then did he start taking off his clothes, neatly folding each item before putting it down on a chair.

I watched. By the time he was totally naked his long penis still hung limp, and I wondered if it was going to be any use to me. Almost his entire body was covered in dark hairs – his chest and back, his arms, legs and buttocks – while his cock was about the largest hairless area on him.

Steve lay down on the bed, propping himself up on one elbow. "Come on," he said. "I've been looking forward to this ever since I first saw you at the airport."

He could have fooled me. He didn't sound at all

enthusiastic, and his prick was equally as lively. I went over to the bed and lay down by his side, and he reached out to run his fingers through my hair.

He must have seen me glancing at his knob, because he said, "Don't worry about that. It's a big one, so it takes longer to get up. And longer to come down. Touch it, go one, hold it."

I did as he asked, grasping it in the palm of my hand, feeling its warmth, sensing it begin to move, the blood pulsing through the thick vein. By the time it was erect, its dimensions had scarcely increased.

One of Steve's hands was fondling my breasts, bringing my nipples to their maximum size, while the fingers of his other hand wriggled through my pubic hairs. I lay on my left side, opening my legs so that his fingers could slide down towards my damp cleft, but I kept a firm grip on his prick, softly pushing the foreskin up towards its tip, then back again. His thumb rubbed gently against my clitoris, the ends of his fingers stroking the edge of my inner labia. We masturbated each other until I could stand it no longer. I had to have him inside of me.

I pulled Steve towards me, raising my right leg over his hips and wrapping it around his waist to hold him as close as possible. He positioned his left leg between my thighs, and his cock slipped easily into my lubricated vagina. And we began to fuck, our bodies soon becoming speckled with sweat and sticking together. Steve kept steadily pumping at the same easy pace, and it was up to me to vary the stroke and pressure on my cunt by rocking faster or slower, either with his movement or against it. The only way I could tell that Steve had come was by his sudden grunt and the way he missed a single beat of his thrust. I hadn't felt his spurts, and when he kept on screwing into me I thought that I'd been wrong, until I realised that he was keeping on for my benefit.

His penis was losing its rigidity, but as compensation he brought his fingers to work on my clit and cunt lips. I'd been taking it easy until then, wanting to hold back and prolong the pleasure. Now I let myself go, allowing the total sensation of orgasm to rocket me into dizzying orbit.

When I came back to earth, Steve had pulled out and was watching me. He smiled. "That was nice," he said. "Thanks."

I nodded, unable to speak.

"I'm not as young as I used to be," Steve continued, "so there doesn't seem to be as much juice as there was. And over the past several days I've almost been drained dry. They're real ball-busters some of those other girls. But I can honestly say you're the best I've had for ages."

I smiled. "Bet you say that you every piece of cunt that comes your way."

"You shouldn't use words like that," Steve chided. "Cunt and fuck. They aren't very ladylike."

I laughed aloud. Lying next by his side, legs wrapped around him, my twat gaping wide open after a good screwing, I certainly didn't feel very ladylike.

"You're right, I suppose," I said, just to keep him happy. "But they're the best words I know, explicit and to the point."

"You'd better get dressed," he said. He rose to his knees and climbed over me. "I've got some more work to do." He began to get dressed. After a few seconds, I also stood up and donned my own clothes. I left while Steve was still dressing.

Three down, five to go.

I was like a kid with a new toy. Now that I'd discovered cocks and finally found out what my cunt was really for, I couldn't wait to try as many different pricks as possible. It was a point of honour that I had to sample all the knobs which had been through the other girls while we'd been in the Caribbean; I couldn't miss out on what they'd been enjoying. And if I succeeded, I'd be top of the league. None of the other three models or the rest of the girls had been honoured by George's tool paying them an intimate visit.

But by the time I returned to the summit of the hill that evening, I still hadn't managed to increase my score. George had brought Debbie, Vanessa and Sandra along, even though he'd promised me the final shot. At that time we didn't know he'd already taken the last picture the previous night. But George whispered to me that he didn't want to seem to have made up his mind in advance, which was why I had to pretend I hadn't been selected and why the other three all had to strip off and pose.

So far we'd all been in an equal number of pictures, either alone or with one or more of the others, and we were in friendly competition to see who'd carry off the prize of being featured in the last picture. I knew I'd won. And I also intended to become the winner when it came to fucking all the men in our group.

While the other girls got prepared and the equipment was lugged up the slope, George and I went back down the hill and called in to see Louis and Celine so we could thank them again. They had visitors, their son and daughter-in-law having arrived from France, but we were invited in for a drink.

"We've come back to do the final shoot," George told them. "The whole crew is here, as well as the other three models."

"You notice how there's no thunderstorm tonight," I said. "That sort of thing only happens to me."

"You don't look any the worse for wear," Louis commented.

I hadn't looked my best the previous night, although in the morning I'd noticed how he'd been studying me.

"Why don't you come on up and watch?" I suggested. "You might find it interesting." My glance took in the rest of his family. "All of you." I looked at George, to make sure I wasn't out of place in issuing this invitation.

"Certainly," George agreed. "You may find it boring, but you're welcome to come along."

Louis nodded thoughtfully. George had told him all about the calendar project after breakfast. Louis had grown more and more interested, and his gaze had lingered even longer on me.

"Go if you wish," Celine told him. She had no idea of the kind of photograph that was being set up.

"I might," Louis muttered, his dark eyes appraising me. He glanced at his son. "Jean Paul?"

The younger man looked puzzled, and Louis spoke to him in French for a few seconds. He was in his early twenties, darkly handsome. Although I'd stared at the promising bulge behind his tight trousers, he had ignored me, possibly because his wife was with him. She was a small girl, with cropped auburn hair; she didn't say a word while we were there, either French or English. Then Jean Paul replied, also in French, shaking his head.

"He's tired after the journey," Louis translated. "Jet lag."

"If you want to come," George said, "please do. You know where we are. If not, I can only thank you again for your hospitality."

"That goes for me, too," I added.

George and I shook hands with everyone, the way the French always do, then headed back up to the top of the rocky hill. The moon was full and high, and the sky was perfectly clear and full of bright sparkling stars. The air was almost still, with only a hint of night wind. It was completely different from yesterday. If the conditions then had been the same as tonight, I'd never have ended up in bed with George. And I'd have missed out on so much.

Within minutes of our arrival, George was in action: arranging for the positioning of the camera, supervising the erection of the lighting boom close to the angle of the moon, checking that the models' hair and faces were properly done. Then he went through the ritual of staring at us all in turn through the viewfinder. Although it wasn't as cold as last night, it wasn't too warm, and standing around in the nude for more than a few minutes became uncomfortable. Whenever we weren't in position, we wore thick robes.

It was while I was posing that I saw Louis. He was standing in the shadows several yards down the slope. I pretended I hadn't noticed him, but as soon as George took my preliminary shots and Vanessa had replaced me, I walked down towards the newcomer. I didn't bother covering myself.

"Hello, Louis," I said, smiling. I held out my hand to him, a sample of what I had to offer.

"Hello," he said, as we shook. I kept hold of his hand, squeezing it.

Louis was trying not to stare, but didn't want to seem rude by not looking at me. He glanced away, but all he could see was another nude girl: at the top of the hill stood Vanessa, legs and arms spread to form an "X" shape.

Letting his hand drop, I turned and followed his gaze. "That's Vanessa," I said. "She's lovely, isn't she?"

"Not as lovely as you, my dear," he told me, which was exactly what I wanted to hear. "You must be cold. Here." He removed his jacket and draped it across my shoulders; it hung just above my crotch.

"Thanks. Yes, I am a bit cold." I moved a pace towards him, and his right arm went around my shoulders. I glanced up at him in the moonlight, at the distinguished grey of his hair, at the symmetry of his oval face.

"Is this what you do all the time?" he asked. "You take your clothes off for photographs?"

"That's right."

"Don't you find it degrading, humiliating?"

I laughed. "Of course not. I like my body, and I like to share it."

His right hand dropped down fractionally, onto the fabric of his jacket directly above the rise of my breast. I didn't react, also leaving the next move to him. I'd chased enough men today. It was my turn to play the submissive role. His hand slipped inside the jacket, finding my breast and the hardness of the dilated nipple, stroking it with his palm. Then he pulled me to him, his lips against mine, his tongue thrusting into my mouth. My tongue responded with equal ardour, my arms clutching his broad back, the jacket falling away from me. Behind us, I heard George calling out instructions to Vanessa.

I drew away from Louis, seizing his arm and pulling him into the darker shadows beneath the tall palm trees which lined the steps to the summit. He leaned back against one of the rough trunks, while my hands found his zip, tugged it down, then reached for what was hidden inside his pants. All the time his hands were sensuously exploring my breasts, his thumbs stroking my nipples.

Then I had his penis in my hand, feeling it swell and grow, stretching upwards, upwards, amazing me with its strength and size. Louis picked me up. He grabbed me by the waist and pressed me up against the tree. I lost my grip on his magnificent cock. As I tried to repossess his flesh, Louis sank down to his knees, nuzzling his face against my cunt, forcing my legs wide apart, turning his face so that he could more easily slip his tongue into the juiciness of my twat.

While his tongue probed and thrust, his lips rubbed and stroked, and his mouth sucked and kissed, I could hardly hold myself upright. The feeling was so sensational that my entire body quivered with delight. I'd only ever had Carole's tongue inside my cunt, but she was a beginner compared to Louis; he seemed to know every one of the tiny pleasure zones in my vagina better than I did. In seconds he was raising me towards ultimate ecstasy, bringing me off far faster than I'd ever come before.

But just as I was about to climax, his tongue withdrew. He leaned away, pulling me over with him. He sat down, then lay on his back, positioning me so that I was kneeling over him, my legs spread across his hips.

I didn't need any instructions. I took hold of his swollen phallus, carefully levering it back so that it pointed upwards, and I lowered myself down onto the stiff flesh, gripping it tightly between the walls of my cunt. Louis's hands came up, caressing my boobs. Then I began to ride him, sliding up and down. It was like masturbating with a dildo – but this was the real thing and infinitely better than any artificial substitute.

My first orgasm came after a few strokes, and I threw myself back, gasping in sheer bliss, panting and groaning.

Then Louis twisted his hips, and I found myself over on my back. He was above me, his cock gliding all the way in, stretching my cunt and venturing deeper than ever. I raised my legs, gripping him around the waist to allow him even greater access.

As he fucked me and I sensed the first quiver of another orgasm, I gazed up at the moon and stars, felt the hardness of the earth beneath my naked body, heard the creak of the palm trees in the slight breeze, smelled the lush aroma of the tropical plants all around us, and tasted the salt in my lover's his sweat where I kissed his throat.

The universe, the world, this island, Louis, myself, we were as one.

NINE

Fucking Louis instead of one of the others played havoc with my schedule the next day, which George had decided would indeed be a holiday, but I did my best. First there was Eddie, one of the guys who did all the fetching and carrying. We were going down to breakfast, the only people in the lift. I pressed the emergency stop, and we did it standing up.

There was no way we could have taken off all our clothes, although Eddie pulled his pants down to his knees and I removed my briefs. After breakfast I met up with Don, who was the main lighting man, and although we were alone in his room he insisted that we stay fully clad. He'd only fuck me if he could shove his cock out of his zip and slide it up inside the elastic of my panties, through into my cunt.

None of the remaining three were available until the afternoon. That was when I cornered Mike, the other lighting guy. We were in the room he shared with Eddie, where I'd fucked fully dressed a few hours earlier. Mike wanted to do it with me on all fours, entering my twat from the rear. So we did. And I was learning all the time.

After dinner I arranged a rendezvous with the second lackey, Graham. Fucking him was pretty normal compared to the previous three: we took off all our clothes, we were lying down, and we did it face to face, Graham on top.

By that time my twat was pretty sore after so much unaccustomed activity, and I half imagined people could hear all that spunk sloshing around inside me as I walked. I hadn't even reached orgasm in two of today's screwing sessions; I was having too much of a good thing, if there ever could be too much . . .

That left only one more. Jack. He was the assistant photographer's assistant, seventeen years old, even younger than me. His long hair was wild and untamed; his complexion was as smooth as a baby's; he'd hardly even begun to shave. I'd listened to the other girls talking about Jack, and he was one of their favourites. He wasn't particularly skilled at fucking, and he always came too soon, but his cock was inexhaustible, always ready for more. Such were the stories I'd heard, and I couldn't wait to discover the truth for myself. The only problem was whether my unpractised cunt could take much more, whether it could keep up with the demands of my lustful body.

But first I had to trace Jack and lure him away from the others. There wasn't very much time left. Word had spread among the rest of the girls that I'd enthusiastically taken up their hobby, and their reaction was ambiguous. Now I was really one of them, but also I was seen as a rival. If I'd asked, they would reluctantly have granted me free access to Jack. I didn't want that, I had to reach him my own way.

I had no chance that final evening, because he'd gone off on the town with the make-up girl. He returned too late for me, because I was exhausted by the previous late night and that day's hectic bouts of fucking. So I went to bed early. Alone. My tender twat was allowed a few hours to recover from the exquisite treatment it had received.

The next morning I found Jack in the room which had been taken over as the studio, packing up all the photographic equipment. He glanced at me as I entered, then continued with what he was doing. I kicked the door shut, walked across the room, then sat down on the bed. I was wearing a short cotton skirt and a translucent blouse, and I leaned back against the wall.

"I'm very busy," he said, not looking up. "I don't have time to fuck you."

His remark took me completely by surprise, but luckily he couldn't have noticed startled my expression. "What makes you think I want you to fuck me?" I asked calmly.

"Why else are you here?"

"I was looking for Steve," I lied.

"He's not here."

"I can see that. I thought he might be back."

"What for?"

"I want him to fuck me," I said.

Jack paused and glanced around at me.

"I want a man to fuck me," I added. "Not a boy."

He shrugged. "That's up to you, but you don't know what you're missing."

"Think a lot of yourself, don't you?"

"With reason." He grinned. "Pity I haven't time to give you a demonstration, but I'm deep enough in the shit already. If I get in any more trouble, I get the sack."

"So? That's not the end of the world."

"I had enough trouble getting this job," Jack told me. "I want to be a photographer, and my brother arranged for me to work with George. He'll murder me if I lose the job."

"Who's going to sack you?"

"George, if I don't get this gear all packed up."

"George?" I said in disbelief. George was too easy going to sack anyone. "Come on."

"You don't know him."

I smiled to myself, because I certainly knew George better than most people; but I said nothing.

"I mean it," said Jack. "He treats you girls okay, but he's a slave driver to any guy he can't fuck. He's a great photographer, though. I want this job."

"You want to replace Steve as George's assistant? You want to be like him in twenty-five years?"

"Steve's a great guy, but he's never had any ambition. Not like me, girl. I'm going places, and George is one of my stepping stones."

I raised my knees up to the level of my shoulders. My skirt slid up my hips, and I opened my legs slightly. I wasn't wearing any panties. Jack knew why I was really here, so there was no point in pretending.

His eyes focused on the blonde curls of my cunt. "I've seen it before, remember? I'm one of the guys always around when you've been posing. So don't waste your time or mine, girl. Your job might be over, but I'm still working."

I ignored him and unfastened my blouse, then slipped my skirt off.

Jack shook his head sadly. "I have to sort out and file all these transparencies. Work is my priority, girl."

I widened my thighs even more, and I knew that he must have been able to see right into my twat through my open labia. Without a word, I started rubbing at my clit with the index finger of my right hand. My left hand went to my breasts, massaging each of them in turn. My eyes narrowed; I tilted back my head; I opened my mouth slightly; and I sighed as I masturbated.

Jack ignored me. His determination would have been quite admirable in most other situations. I was convinced that he wanted to fuck me. He could easily have spared a few minutes. But he was deliberately avoiding me, perhaps as an exercise in masochism. Whatever the reason, I didn't intend to let him get away with it. I wasn't going to be made a fool of, flaunting myself in front of him like this while he took no notice.

Under such circumstances, I could have stroked my clitoris for all eternity and never come off, so I stopped and climbed down from the bed. I was tempted to leave, but that would have been an admission of defeat. I was here for one thing: Jack's cock. And I intended to have it, one way or another.

"Perhaps I can help you," I suggested.

"If you want," he said, shrugging. He stood by a table, sorting through the transparencies scattered across its surface. He was looking at them all, marking them off against a list, then slotting them into different boxes.

I moved over to stand next to him.

"I have to check the numbers here, see?" he told me.

But that wasn't quite the help I had in mind. I rested my hand on the table, moving even closer to Jack, my hip touching his. Then my hand brushed one of the transparencies onto the floor, and it fell under the table. I bent down to retrieve it, and I saw the unmistakable shape of an erection pressing against the fabric of Jack's jeans: certain proof that he wasn't as disinterested in me as he pretended.

I crawled under the table, but it wasn't the transparency I was after. Kneeling on the ground, my naked buttocks resting on my heels, I faced Jack. My head was on the same level as his groin, and I reached up for his belt. Jack made no protest as I undid the buckle and unfastened the top button of his jeans. Then I carefully unzipped him, tugging at the soft fabric of the faded denims until they fell and left his tanned legs bare. His leg muscles tensed and relaxed slightly as he leaned further across the table. He carried on sorting through the transparencies.

He was wearing a pair of tight black jockey shorts, and the end of his cock poked up through the elastic at the top. I stroked the full length of his penis, from balls to glans, with the tip of my right index finger, then squeezed it gently through the cotton of his underwear with my hand. The fingers of my left hand fondled his testicles through the material, which was damp with sweat. After a few seconds, I let go with both hands and leaned back, wondering if Jack's determination to ignore me was more powerful than his sexual instincts.

I didn't have to wait too long before one of his hands reached down beneath the surface of the table, searching blindly for me. My head darted out, and I seized one of his fingers in my mouth, holding it firmly but not painfully between my teeth. Then I let go, instead sucking it with my lips, drawing my mouth back and licking the finger with my tongue, letting him know what else I could do . . . if he wanted.

And he wanted it. As I withdrew my attention from his finger, his hands went to his black underwear, pushing it down over his hips, his thighs, his knees, his shins, then using his feet to push off both his jeans and his pants.

For the first time I could see his penis fully. It was so elegant and beautiful, projecting blatantly upwards, the hairy sack of his testicles drawn up tightly beneath. No wonder the other girls so admired Jack; his cock was as flawless as he was. I could hardly wait to taste it, to feel it in my mouth. That was something I hadn't done yet, and the idea of fellatio had never seemed very attractive. I'd heard the other girls discussing blow-jobs, and I'd considered the theory over the past two days, ever since my ideas had been so radically altered. Until now I hadn't seen a prick which appealed to me, but Jack's knob was so absolutely irresistible that I moistened my lips and leaned forwards to kiss it.

I started at the base of the shaft, then kissed it almost to the top, my lips feeling the blood pulse through it. Then I slid my mouth down again, my tongue flicking wetly all around the soft hairy skin of the scrotum. I opened my mouth as wide as I could, drawing in the testicles, washing them with my saliva, before letting them loose again.

My hands were on Jack's buttocks, and I could feel the movement from his torso above as he tried to continue with his work. But I didn't care about the rest of his body, all I wanted was his cock. My tongue returned its loving attention to that perfect flesh, one of my hands coming around to hold it steady and at a more accessible angle as I licked and sucked its length, gradually, inevitably, working up towards the purple glans and its hidden promise.

I ran my tongue around the ridge of the swollen head, around and around. Then I licked at the domed tip and probed into the tiny slit to discover the first drop of fluid. When my mouth retreated, a thin trail of spunk, as slender as a spider's web, linked my tongue and Jack's cock. Leaning forward again, my lips took over from my tongue, following the delicious contours of the glans, and my mouth slowly began to draw the length of his tool across my tongue and towards my throat.

I licked and sucked, slurping hungrily. Jack's penis felt so good in my mouth, performing oral sex for him was almost as satisfying as having a tongue in my own twat. I was enjoying giving him pleasure, because I could imagine how much he was liking what I did. And although I was concentrating on my task, I became aware that Jack was no longer even pretending to sort through his transparencies. His thighs were tense, his hips pushed forward, encouraging me to swallow him even more.

The end of his cock brushed against the soft flesh at the roof of my mouth, and I bent my neck a little, so that I could take even more of him into me. But my mouth simply wasn't big enough, although by thrusting out my tongue I could reach the base of his shaft. I allowed his dick to slide a few of inches out of my mouth, my tongue lapping at its throbbing length. Before Jack's cock could slip totally free, I sucked it back in again, one hand gripping its base and feeding it into my mouth, while the other cupped the testicles and gave fingertip stimulation.

After a few irregular movements, I established a proper rhythm, sucking in most of the knob, then blowing it out again. My tongue worked on the tip as it slipped into my mouth, while my lips gripped tight as it slid in and out. In and out, in and out, in and out . . .

And Jack's hips began to jerk to and fro, forcing his cock even deeper into my mouth. Then he became abruptly still. Although I knew what this meant, his first gush of semen took me by surprise. It splashed against the back of my throat, almost causing me to gag, and I tried to pull away. But Jack was holding himself into me as he ejaculated, and my mouth was filled with his pulsing spunk. I managed to lean back, tugging at his cock with my hands, and his final spurts dribbled down my fingers.

Then the door opened, and George walked in. He stopped in his tracks, staring at Jack, then lowering his head so that he could see who was under the table.

"Hello, sweetie," he said to me.

I could feel Jack's semen heavy in my mouth, taste its rich texture on my tongue. I swallowed.

"Hello, George," I replied.

George stood up straight. He stared at Jack, his eyes studying the lower half of his anatomy, and he half smiled. "Glad to see you're still working," he remarked. "You've got about an hour." He glanced down at me. "That goes for you, too, sweetie. We've got to check in at the airport in two hours." He turned and went out again.

I crawled from under the table.

Jack was watching me, and he exhaled noisily. "If that had been anyone else but you under there," he said, "I'd have been sacked. For some reason you're George's favourite."

"Then you ought to be grateful I was here," I told him. "How long will it take you to finish? If I help you."

"About half an hour," Jack told me.

"Then you owe me a favour, don't you?" I said, gazing down at his still erect penis. I noticed the back of my right hand, speckled with creamy white drops, and I raised my arm so that Jack could see them as well. I put my hand to my mouth, and I licked it clean.

Jack nodded slightly, trying not to smile. But he failed. "I suppose so," he agreed. He looked over towards the bed, and I went to lie down.

The other girls had been right. Jack might have been a fast shooter, but he had staying power. And he was so full of energy, rolling me over and over, bending me into so many various athletic positions, that it was more like a bout of unarmed combat than fucking. He even managed to come again while we were screwing. But all that mattered was the magnificent climax which he gave me – as well as all the minor but delightful orgasmic ripples which radiated from my cunt to engulf every particle of my being.

After a few minutes' rest to recharge our drained bodies and allow the sweat to evaporate from our steaming flesh, I helped Jack finish sorting out all the transparencies which George had taken during the fortnight.

"How would you like to be in the movies?" he asked me, as we checked off the list.

"Aren't you supposed to say that to me before you fuck me senseless?" I said, grinning. "The old casting couch story."

He stopped what he was doing and looked directly at me. "I'm serious," he told me.

"Go on, I'm listening."

"You're the best looking girl here, and my brother is always searching for good looking girls," Jack explained. "I mentioned him before. He's the one who got me this job with George. Colin, that's his name. He's a photographer, too, but he's also into film making. Corporate videos, that sort of thing, as well as more interesting stuff. He asked me to keep an eye out for likely talent. And I think you fit the bill perfectly. Are you interested?"

"Yeah," I said. "Maybe." It sounded intriguing, and I didn't have anything lined up when we got back. I wondered if Colin would be anything like his brother. But meanwhile I still had Jack. And his cock.

"Hurry up." I gestured towards the transparencies. "Maybe there'll be time for another fuck."

And there was.

I tilted the bottle of cola into my mouth, allowing the contents to pour down my throat, letting some of it trickle out from my lips and drip down my chin, dropping onto my bare breasts. My hand massaged the liquid into the upper curve of my boobs, my fingers moving lower to circle the nipple, caressing it to even greater magnitude.

My hand continued its expedition across my body, stroking the tanned flesh of my ribcage, sliding over my stomach, gliding down to the curls of my crotch as I spread my legs. Then my other hand descended the same route, holding the glass bottle. I poured a generous measure of cola over my blonde pubic hairs, rubbing it in until they were sopping wet. I stroked the inside of my thigh with the neck of the bottle, pushing it higher and higher towards the lips of my cunt, lightly brushing its mouth between my wet hairs.

I breathed heavily, leaning back against the wall and thrusting my hips forward. There was no way that I could possibly control my desires. I rubbed the round neck of the bottle against my clitoris, twisting it between the labia.

"Stop, stop, stop!" yelled Colin. "Cut, I mean."

He stared at the ceiling in despair, then wiped non-existent sweat from his face with palm of his hand. He was a better actor than I was, not that this was saying much. Colin wasn't as handsome as his brother, not quite so tall, but more thickly-set. And whereas Jack's face was as smooth as an infant's, Colin had a ragged beard. I'd spent the night we arrived back from the Caribbean with Jack. The next day he introduced me to his brother, and so the following night was devoted to Colin. Two days later I was working for him.

"Sorry," I muttered, although I wasn't. I kept on stroking the bottle against my swollen clit.

"It won't do," Colin told me. He turned to the video crew. "Take five," he said, then he walked towards me.

"Why are you so . . . so hot all the time?" he demanded.

"I just can't get enough, I suppose."

He shook his head in disbelief. "You wore me out this morning. What makes you so inexhaustible?"

I shrugged. Colin might once have been as potent as his younger brother, although his knob could never have tasted so delicious, but that was several years ago. Now he could only keep his cock up until he climaxed; after that he was no use whatsoever. All he'd done was to bring me up to a certain level – and by then I simply wanted more, more, more. Women can keep on screwing far longer than any mere male, but like all men Colin was unable to accept this. If he was sexually satiated, he didn't see why the same shouldn't be true of me.

"Take that bottle out of your twat, huh?" he said.

I did as he asked. It was a poor substitute for a firm prick, but it was better than nothing.

"If you want to bring yourself off, go ahead. Maybe then you'll have cooled down for the next scene. I've already told you, we're making a video for the whole family. Or almost. Something that can be distributed and sold without any problems. This is make-believe sex. Just girls, no men. The viewer is the only male we're concerned with. He's the guy who imagines that he's fucking all you nubile young ladies. We can't have you shoving a bottle up your twat. It isn't very subtle, I know, but the viewer has to think of the bottle as his own cock. And we like to leave a little for his imagination. It's okay putting it in your mouth, the stuff pouring out like overflowing spunk. It might be obvious, but it isn't as blatant as you fucking yourself with that bottle. See?"

I nodded, hardly listening. The neck of the bottle was between my labia again, gliding against my clitoris. I'd known what we were meant to be doing, but whenever I felt the urge there was no way I could ignore it. Such was the case now, and I moaned as I gave the bottle a final twist to achieve a very satisfying orgasm.

Colin ran his fingers through his hair, turning away and shaking his head.

Apart from the camera crew, there were a number of other men present. And unlike the calendar shooting sessions in the Caribbean, I suspected that most of them had no reason to be there. All they did was watch. I half suspected that Colin made as much money by charging fees to these voyeurs as he did for making his video erotica.

Our location was the changing rooms of a local football team, so it was a safe bet that Colin was paying off the hire fee by allowing a few officials in as spectators – to witness a different kind of sporting activity.

There were two other girls in this scene as well as me, Sharon and Lena. We were meant to be part of a women's soccer team. (Colin's budget wouldn't stretch to eleven of us.) We did the kind of things women did together after a match – meaning the kind of things men liked to imagine girls did – removing one another's muddy shirts and shorts, then washing each other's breasts and buttocks in the showers.

As Colin had said, no men were involved, only girls. And sex between girls was okay, because that didn't represent a threat to any red-blooded macho male. Lesbianism was good clean harmless fun, so long as we didn't go too far. And that included going too far with ourselves as well, as I'd just learned.

My fellow actresses were very attractive and after concentrating so much energy on fucking men, it was nice for me to be able to see naked female flesh again. And unlike in the Caribbean, I could touch as well as look.

It was true that Colin had given me a good screwing before we arrived here, but after a morning's proximity to two other gorgeous girls – watching and helping them strip off, then frolicking in the showers with them – it was only to be expected that I'd reach a peak of randiness which had to be satiated.

"Never mind," said Colin. "We'll be able to use most of that and edit out the bit where you start screwing yourself. Now let's try the rest of that scene. You've come out of the shower first, had your drink, then Sharon comes out. She's all wet, and you give her what's left of your cola. Perhaps we'd better get her another bottle. She won't want to drink that one after it's been up your cunt. You two do your stuff, and then Lena arrives." He nodded in encouragement. "You're doing fine," he said.

"Good," I replied, although I wasn't sure how I could have been doing otherwise. None of this took any particular skill or talent. All Colin wanted was bodies, naked female bodies, young and pretty. I, of course, fitted the bill perfectly. We didn't have to act, didn't have any lines to speak. There was nothing to go wrong. Except when I got too carried away with what I was doing. But I didn't care. I was enjoying myself. I'd liked posing for George's camera, and here I had the opportunity to be even more of an exhibitionist.

I remembered how a few weeks earlier George had wanted to take some cunt shots of me and I'd refused. But compared to what I was doing now, the idea of explicit nude photographs was so tame.

Colin shouted for order and he brought me another bottle of cola as a replacement. It was half-full, I noticed. He muttered something about continuity. Because there was no dialogue and therefore no sound, Colin was able to give us our instructions as we went along. A music track would be added later, he'd informed me.

Sharon went back into the shower to make herself all wet again. She had a thick mane of blonde hair, but it was bleached, a fact which might not have been so obvious if her pubic hairs hadn't been jet black. Yet there was something very alluring about her two-tone design, almost like having two girls in one. Lena's hair wasn't its natural colour either, being streaked in reds and blues and greens. Her cunt hairs were light brown, which was a clue to her real shade. She was very slim, with hips and buttocks like a boy's. But she had very generous tits with lovely dark nipples, which was obviously why she'd been hired for the film. I'd hardly been able to cover one of her boobs with both hands, while Sharon's palms had been busy with Lena's other soapy breast.

"Let's go," Colin commanded.

I resumed my position on the bench, the bottle clutched against my thigh. Sharon appeared from the shower room, naked, shaking drops of water from her hair. She walked over and stood above me, rubbing at her breasts with her hands as if to dry herself. I passed her my cola, and she held it against her mouth, her tongue licking at the neck of the bottle.

"Good," called Colin. "Now put it in your mouth and let some spill out."

Sharon obeyed, doing exactly the same as I'd done earlier. I didn't think she was doing it quite right. She seemed to treat it as just a bottle, not as if it were a cock. But Colin seemed happy enough.

"Good," he said again. "Now swap places."

I stood up, and Sharon sat down.

"Go behind her and start drying her hair. Lean down over her, let your tits brush against her. Good. Good."

I followed my instructions, towelling Sharon's wet hair and bending over her, my naked breasts rubbing against her bare shoulders. She closed her eyes, her head swaying luxuriously from side to side. We carried on like this for a while, then Colin yelled for Lena. She entered, water coursing off her nude flesh. I moved around to the front of Sharon, going down on my haunches in front of her to dry her legs. Lena stood behind Sharon, who leaned back and raised her arms to cup Lena's big damp boobs.

I raised one of Sharon's legs, pulling her thighs apart, while behind me the cameraman came closer so that he could film her pink twat. I stared at the inviting cunt lips, at the tiny glistening ridge of flesh that was Sharon's clitoris. I slid my hands higher up her thigh, rubbing with the towel.

"Good, good," said Colin, who stood close to the cameraman. "Sharon, pour your drink down over your breasts. Lena, rub her tits. Good. Sharon, move the bottle lower. Keep letting it trickle out. That's right. Now pour it all over your snatch. Good."

The cola ran through Sharon's pubic hairs, some of it finding the shallow valley which led to her cunt, dripping into the folds of her labia, while more of it flowed down the inside of her thighs.

Without waiting for Colin's direction, I decided to improvise. I leaned forwards, bending my head, and began to lick the liquid from Sharon's thighs, my tongue snaking out to lap up every drop.

"Good!" Colin said in encouragement. "That's the stuff!"

My mouth moved higher up Sharon's thigh, meeting the trickle of cola, until my tongue was only an inch away from the moist lips of her cunt. I eased myself nearer, half expecting Colin to yell at me. But before he realised what I was doing, my lips were against Sharon's labia, my hands gripping her hips so that she couldn't pull away. Then I thrust my tongue deep into her cleft, rubbing up and down the walls of her vulva.

Sharon twisted, trying to get free. She cried out in protest, and I was also aware of Colin shouting at me. But I didn't care. After a few seconds of frantic licking, expecting to be hauled away from my prize any moment, I felt Sharon's fingers running through my hair, then pressing against the back of my head, urging me deeper and deeper into her. Her hips jerked against my face as her whole body wriggled and writhed.

It had been a long time since I'd done this; Sharon was only the second girl ever to have known my tongue. My own twat was damp, eager for a tongue inside it, and I wondered what my chances were.

Then Sharon climaxed, almost screaming out in triumph as she peaked. My tongue lapped thirstily at the sweet mixture of cola and cunt juice. I pulled my mouth back a fraction, gently kissing her labia a final time. Then I withdrew and stood up, wiping my lips with my fingertips.

I looked at Sharon, but she stared guiltily at the ground and wouldn't meet my eyes. I turned towards Colin and shrugged apologetically.

He rolled his eyes in despair. "There's only one solution for this," he said.

"What's that?"

"You'll have to go into hardcore, that's all."

"Hardcore?" I asked, not sure what it meant. I was still very naive. After all, I'd only lost my virginity a few days earlier.

"Porn," Colin told me. "Films where you can fuck and suck to your heart's content – and your cunt's."

I wasn't sure whether he was joking or not. Sex films were all pretence. Surely no one made movies of people actually fucking . . .

TEN

Colin assured me that he was entirely serious. He didn't make hardcore films himself, but he insisted on introducing me to someone who did. I had no intention of ever screwing on film. There was no way I'd agree to make fuck movies, but I was interested in hearing about them. A rendezvous was arranged for the following evening.

"This is Murphy," said Colin, introducing us.

Murphy was casually but expensively dressed, like a lawyer or accountant on his day off, although a lawyer or accountant probably wouldn't hair halfway down his back.

"How's business?" he asked Colin, when he returned from the bar with the drinks. We sat in the far corner, away from everyone else.

"Okay," Colin said, shrugging, not wanting to let Murphy know how well he was doing. He'd bought a brand new sports car last week, but parked it away from the bar so that Murphy wouldn't see it. "You?"

"I survive," Murphy nodded, and I guessed that he must have been making at least as much money as Colin. He looked at me. "So you'd like to be a porn star?"

"I'm not sure," I said, and I wasn't.

Murphy glanced sharply at Colin.

"She's a natural," Colin assured him. "She just needs talking into it."

"You get paid for fucking," Murphy said to me. "The best of both worlds. What more could you want? You get to fuck lots of guys with big pricks. Isn't that what every girl wants?"

He shrugged, as though he'd explained everything. "You've seen porn films, you know what they're like."

"No," I said, "I haven't."

"Not even mine?" Murphy pretended to be astonished.

I laughed. "I don't really believe there are such films. People fucking each other? Who appears in them?"

"Girls like you," Murphy said. "You've got a good body, so you should make the most of it. You'll be well paid, far better than you would be in most other jobs. What else would you rather do, huh? Work in a shop? A factory? An office? Who needs that? You only live once – so live, that's my motto."

"But what if someone saw me?" I asked.

"That's the idea." Murphy smiled, because he was aware of exactly what meant. "Someone you know, that's what you mean. So what? Why should you care? I hear you've done nude photographic work, this isn't much different."

I didn't agree. Fucking on film was a million miles away from posing topless for a calendar, or even making that girlie video for Colin.

"I know exactly what sort of girl you are," Murphy continued, staring straight into my eyes. "You're the type who doesn't give a damn, nothing bothers you. You'll do anything for a dare. You're not fettered by the invisible chains which bind everyone else. You do what you want, you do it your own way, no one orders you about. You're today's girl, totally free and independent. You're young, you've got your whole life in front of you, and you ought to try everything you can. Seize each opportunity, because there's nothing to lose. A moment lost is gone forever. You're the most important person in the world, and you know it. That's why you don't mind being photographed nude. You're saying to everyone: look at me, I'm wonderful. And if they don't like what they see, tough shit. You're unique, you're you, you've got your own body, and you do with it exactly as you please. You like people to see you, to watch you. You're a natural exhibitionist. I've heard all about the wet T-shirt competition. You're at your best when you rely on your raw animal instincts and lusts. You like people watching you. You enjoyed sucking that other girl in Colin's film even more than you would have done in privacy, because you like people to watch. You've got so much to offer. It's the same with fucking. Society says that should be private, between two people. But why only two? And why should it be done in secret? I'm offering you the chance to fuck as many men and girls as you can handle. No one will be telling you to stop, quite the opposite. I can simply look at you and know you'll be a sensation. I don't have to fuck you myself. I don't even have to see you in the nude. As Colin said, you're a natural. Do you want to do it?"

I took a sip at my drink, sighed, and then nodded. "I'll give it a try," I said. After such a sales pitch, how could I refuse?

"Fine." Murphy picked up his glass of scotch at last and drained it in one gulp. He looked at Colin. "Ten o'clock tomorrow morning, you know where." He stood up.

"That's it?" I asked.

"That's it," agreed Murphy

"What about money?" I asked him.

"If you're good, and I'm sure you are, then you'll make plenty," Murphy told me, and he turned and walked away.

"You going to do it?" Colin asked, after Murphy had vanished through the door.

"Why are you so anxious to get rid of me?" I wanted to know.

"I'm only thinking of your career." But he couldn't manage to hide his smile.

"You want to see me on screen and say to your mates, 'I used to fuck her.' That's it, isn't it?"

Colin took a mouthful of beer instead of answering.

"Why don't you make hardcore yourself?" I asked.

"It's a lot of hassle. Finding the right people, or any people, problems with distribution. Anyway, when I see the guys in those films it gives me an inferiority complex." He grinned. "And I get jealous of them fucking all those beautiful girls."

"But you don't mind me being fucked?"

Colin shrugged. "You've been fucked before, you'll be fucked again. I know you can't get enough, that I'm just another cock to you. We've known each other a few days, we've both enjoyed it, but we aren't exactly Romeo and Juliet."

We said goodbye later that evening. It took all night.

The next day I made my first porn film.

I was very nervous when I arrived, not sure what I'd be letting myself in for, but Colin drove me to the place and went in with me. We found Murphy, and then Colin left. He'd said he didn't want to stick around, that he wasn't needed. His final advice was, "Do what comes naturally."

"This is Polly," said Murphy, introducing me to a voluptuous brunette in her mid-twenties, dressed in a pink trouser suit. "She's the star of the show."

We said hello to each other. Polly eyed me suspiciously, sizing me up as a rival.

"Show her the ropes, Polly, will you?" asked Murphy. Without waiting for a reply he walked away, shouting to the guy who was rigging up the lights.

We were on the top floor of a large isolated house on the outskirts of the city. There was a big recreation room at the end of the landing, but it had been transformed into a bedroom, its centrepiece being a water bed. I'd heard of them, but I'd never seen one until now.

I looked at Polly, and she smiled thinly. "Your first time?" she asked. When I nodded, her smile broadened. "I can always tell." She beckoned me to follow her, and we went to sit down on a sofa in the corner of the room. "They always say that the first time is the worst, and that's probably true. I've seen dozens of girls work for only a day, or even just a few hours or minutes. But there's nothing to it if you like cock. Do you?"

I nodded, although I wasn't so certain any longer. What if I was expected to fuck someone I didn't like? There was no reason why I had to do anything I didn't want to. I could simply get up and walk out if I wished.

Polly was still smiling secretly, as though she knew something I didn't – which was almost certainly the case, because she'd done this so often before and I hadn't.

"Murphy's a good guy to work with," Polly told me. "But he expects a lot from us. Know what I mean?"

I shrugged, because I didn't know.

"It's the girls who make any film," Polly continued. "A girl who knows her job can make the guys look really great, but the best stud it the world can only shine if he's got a girl who knows her job. All the guys have to offer is a few inches of hard cock. And don't believe these myths about big cocks being the best. I've tried them all; I've worked all over the world. Twelve inch cocks? I've fucked them and I've sucked them. But they're freaks, like women with sixty-inch tits. They're useless, believe me. So heavy that they can't even stand up straight. That's the whole mythology of sex – bigger must be better. Remember that old saying, 'It ain't what you got, it's what you do with it'? It's true, believe me."

Polly stared at me, at my blonde hair, the curves of my breasts, my long legs. She was making a point, even though she was pretending to be friendly: I might be the sort of girl most guys would like to fuck, but no one should judge by appearances. When it came down to reality, I wouldn't able to handle this film.

But she was scared of me, I realised, worried that because I was younger and prettier I was going to steal the limelight. She had good reason to worry: I was better than her; I was better than anyone; I was better than everyone.

"You must have made a lot of these films," I said.

"That's right," she nodded.

"Been making them for years," I added, smiling as though to take the edge off my words. "I can learn a lot from you, Polly."

She hesitated, not sure exactly of what I meant.

"You know," I continued, "I've never seen a porn film? I'll be making one before I've even seen one."

"Same thing happened to me," said Polly. "So we have that in common. But of course there's a lot more being made these days. In the old days . . ." She paused, grinning. "Before my time, you realise. They're a lot better than they used to be, better production values and plots, real motivation and characterisation."

I expected her to smile again, but she didn't; she was absolutely serious. She seemed to believe every word she was staying, as though she was some superstar talking about her latest multi-million dollar Hollywood feature. But if Polly was happy in her work, then that was the main thing.

"Can you tell me something about this film?" I asked. "What's happening? What am I supposed to do?"

"You just do what Murphy says," Polly told me. "We filmed half of it yesterday. This is my house, my bedroom." She gestured towards the water bed, and for a moment I thought she meant that she really lived here; then I realised that she was discussing her film role. "I'm all alone in bed, amusing myself with my vibrator. I've forgotten that the decorators are downstairs. One of them sees me and comes into the room. We fuck. Then the other guy comes along and joins in. Usual kind of thing with two guys and one girl."

I tried to imagine what she meant by that; I half guessed, but I wasn't totally sure.

"That's as far as we got yesterday," Polly continued. "Nick and Alex had to recuperate overnight. That's another thing about guys, what I was saying earlier. Once they've shot their load, they're useless."

"Can't they fake it?"

"Fake it?" Polly laughed. "This is the real thing."

"But they can pretend to have orgasms, can't they?"

"There's no pretending because—" She broke off, then nodded in realisation. "I forgot, you've never seen one of these films. There's always a guy who has a real climax. He pulls his cock out and shoots his load all over the girl. It's one of the traditions of the genre." She smiled. "Perhaps to prove it's the real thing, not simulated sex. As if the camera angles aren't explicit enough. Male orgasm can be faked, of course. I've seen various tricks with white of egg, but it's never the same as a throbbing cock spurting out its spunk." She licked her lips, grinning, then put her hands on her waist. "Sometimes I wonder if I should swallow so much come; it's meant to be very high in calories." Then she looked at me again. "At least you shouldn't have that problem for a while."

"You were telling me about the film," I prompted. I wanted to be forewarned. Two guys at once? Withdrawing and letting their semen shoot out? What a waste of spunk!

"That's right," said Polly. "Where was I? Oh, yes. The two guys had to take the night off so they can do it again. I think we'll carry on where we left off. Then you appear on the scene, and they fuck you as well. You're my neighbour or something. You don't have many lines."

"Lines?" I asked. "I have to speak?"

"Of course you have to speak. This is a proper film, with dialogue and a script. But most of the talking is stuff like 'I want your big cock in my mouth', and 'That's so great', and 'Oh-oh-oh-oh-oh'. Murphy will tell you what to say. In any case, your mouth will be full quite a lot of the time. What are you like at giving head?"

"Alright, I suppose."

"It doesn't really matter," said Polly. "You've just got to look as though you're good. It doesn't matter what the guy thinks. In fact, it's best not to be too good or else he'll come too quick. In movies it's mostly pretence. You've got to pretend you're getting the best fuck of your life, that whatever happens you're really enjoying yourself. When in doubt, smile. Always let the camera get a good look at what you're doing or what's being done to you, no matter what contortions you're going through. Let them see your tongue working on the guy's cock, let them see his shaft rubbing against your clit. You must keep your hair away from the side of your face, because that might obstruct the view of you gobbling away. And you've always got to open your legs really wide."

I nodded as I absorbed all this information. It seemed that Polly was being a real professional, passing on all the tips she knew because she wanted the film to be as good as possible. Or possibly she was hoping to put me off, that I might quit the set because there was too much for me to know and learn. But if I took everything step by step, there would be no problem. I could handle it.

"Let's go down to the kitchen for a coffee," Polly suggested. We got up and went downstairs, where she ground some fresh coffee and filled the percolator. We'd only been in the kitchen a couple of minutes when two men came in through the door. "Nick and Alex," she told me, and I looked at the two guys who were going to fuck me.

Nick was in his early twenties, Alex a decade older. Both were almost six feet tall, with dark hair. Alex had a moustache, while Nick's bare arms were both tattooed in blue and red. On his right arm a dagger impaled a heart which dripped blood, while the left showed a naked girl with a snake wrapped around her body.

"You'll see more of Nick's tattoos soon," Polly told me, as we sat around the table and drank coffee.

The other three were talking about where they planned to go on holiday, but I hardly spoke. I didn't know what to say. We didn't have to go through the ritual dialogue the way men and women always do when they're evaluating possible sexual partners, because our fucking was inevitable.

As I watched Nick and Alex, I felt a tingle in my cunt, and I realised that I was eagerly anticipating what was to happen. I'd never met them before, but soon they'd both be screwing me. Or perhaps only one would have me, I wasn't sure what Murphy had planned. I tried to decide which one I'd prefer. They were both muscular and rugged, and I'd probably have been attracted to them under other circumstances. Knowing for certain that we'd fuck took away any mystery and suspense, but I could do without that. All I wanted was the basic: a solid length of cock . . . or even two cocks.

Murphy entered the kitchen and nodded hello to his male actors. "Okay, gang. We're ready for you now. We continue with the scene where Alex and Nick are fucking Polly, so get up there and strip off. I'll be with you in a moment."

The other three left, and Murphy poured himself a cup of coffee. "All set?" he asked me.

I nodded. "What happens," Murphy said, "is that you come into the room and see what's going on. You're surprised but also intrigued, watching your friend being shafted by those two guys. You don't want to watch, but you can't help it. You get excited and start touching yourself up. You want to join in. But then you're seen, and you try to escape. The two guys run after you. They chase you around the house and catch you. But you want to be caught. They carry you back to the bedroom. They strip off your clothes and start to stimulate you. And you like it. Then one of them begins to fuck you, while the other continues screwing Polly again." He shrugged. "That's the story so far. We'll take it from there, do as much as we can with two girls and two guys. Any questions?"

"Polly said something about learning lines."

"You needn't worry about that. Anything else?"

I shook my head, even though I could think of several questions. The answers would all be supplied if I waited to see what happened.

"Shall we go?" Murphy said. We went out of the kitchen and up the stairs, pausing outside one of the rooms on the landing. "I want you to get changed," he told me.

"What you're wearing isn't really suitable. There's some other clothes in there, things more glamorous and easy to rip off. Whenever you're ready, come on out and see what's happening."

I went into the bedroom, closing the door behind me. I hadn't given much thought to my outfit, having imagined that I wouldn't be wearing any costume, and so I'd arrived in just a pair of sandals, loose slacks and a baggy sweater. To save time stripping off, I hadn't bothered with any underwear, but Murphy had made up for that with what he'd provided for me.

I peeled off my other clothes, then began to dress up. All of the undergarments were black – a front-fastening bra, cut so low that my nipples weren't covered, a pair of crotchless frilly panties, and a suspender belt for the pair of black seamed stockings. The cotton skirt was bright red, knee-length, fastened down the right side by a row of buttons; I only buttoned half of them, leaving plenty of thigh exposed. My white blouse was almost transparent, with a plunging neckline; it was held together by a single bow just above my breasts, so that it hung loose and showed my bare stomach. The outfit was completed by a pair of black high-heeled leather ankle boots.

Once I was dressed, I combed my hair and checked my make-up. I left the bedroom and went towards the room where they were filming.

I stopped in the doorway, staring at the astonishing scene. A group of men were clustered around the water bed: Murphy, two cameramen, the sound engineer, and two technicians whose purpose I couldn't work out. Polly and Nick and Alex were at work on the bed. Nick was lying on his back, and Polly was stretched out on top, facing him, while Alex was above Polly. Nick's cock was in her cunt, while Alex's prick was rear-ending her.

Murphy was giving directions to his stars, then he noticed I was by the door. The crew all backed away so that one of the cameraman could get an angle which would show me beyond the bed, watching the three performers fucking. I was sent out and had to return through the doorway, while the other cameraman moved towards me for a reaction shot of my astounded expression. It wasn't difficult for me to look surprised, because I was.

I'd never seen other people fucking, although Colin's bed had been surrounded by mirrors and I'd found it fascinating to watch myself in action from various different angles. But to see Polly sandwiched between Nick and Alex, a thick knob driving into each of her lower orifices, was a strange spectacle. I watched, my heartbeat increasing, my skin prickling with sweat. I felt timid now, deliciously menaced by the thought of Nick and Alex both fucking me at once.

I began touching my breasts with one hand, while the other slid up my thigh and began stroking my pubis.

"That's fine," Murphy told me. "Now we take a shot of the bed, with one of the guys realising you're there. They both see you and chase after you. You flee out of the room, along the landing, down the stairs. But before you can get to the front door, they catch you."

It seemed to take ages to film the chase scene. The two cameramen took shots from different positions as I repeatedly ran away, down the stairs, rushing for the exit. Nick and Alex pursued me, their jutting cocks like some kind of threatening weapon. They both had long thick penises, essential for their roles as porn studs. After a couple of takes, their pricks began to wilt and they had to stroke and rub at them to maintain their erections.

I dashed out of the bedroom and sprinted along the corridor, only arriving at the top of the stairs by the time my two pursuers had reached the door. I raced down the steps, hearing them rushing after me. Nick hurdled the rail at the top of the landing and was halfway down the steps in a single leap, while Alex took the stairs three at once. By the time I reached the hall, they were almost upon me.

Nick lunged forward, grabbing at my skirt, tugging so hard that he pulled the thing off as I twisted away. Then Alex's hands grasped the front of my blouse, ripping the garment from me, so that I was left with only my scant undies as covering.

I squealed with delight, and they both laughed as they grabbed me. Together, they half-carried, half-dragged me back up the stairs, into the bedroom, and flung me down onto the water bed by Polly's side.

Polly grabbed my arms, pinning me down, while Alex pulled off my boots but kept a secure hold on my legs. Nick went to work on me, his hands exploring my vital areas, my breasts and then my crotch. He could reach my nipples and my cunt without even needing to tug away my flimsy garments. He tongued my nipples, while his fingertips delved through my blonde curls and deep into my moist cleft. His mouth moved lower, lower, taking the place of his hand; his teeth plucked at the slit in my panties; his tongue thrust into my twat. I no longer had to act, to pretend that I was being aroused. Because I really was.

Then Polly leaned over me, her lips pushing against mine, and I opened my mouth to admit her probing tongue – and she wasn't acting either, because there was no way that the camera could see her tongue at work against mine. She was the first female I'd kissed since Carole. As she let go of my arms, my hands came up to caress her breasts, feeling the hardness of her nipples against my palms. She pulled her face away, her mouth closing on my right breast, gently sucking on the nipple and stroking it with her tongue. I'd never had two tongues working on me at the same time, and the effect was electric, bringing me towards orgasm more than twice as fast as a single mouth could do.

Alex had let go of my legs by now, and he moved around the other side of the bed so that he could kiss my lips. While he attended to my mouth and Carole sucked my boobs, Nick continued to lick my cunt and softly nibble my clitoris. I began to writhe again, but in ecstasy rather than in any pretended attempt at freedom.

I was aware of Murphy issuing instructions. But even if I'd heard him say anything to me, I wouldn't have been able to react. All I could do was lie helplessly at the mercy of the other three and their skilled tongues.

But before I could reach the ultimate height, I was left all alone. The three of them pulled away. Alex and Polly were fondling each other above me. He stroked her breasts while she rubbed the length of his prick between her hands. Then they tumbled over together, Polly on her back, and Alex plunged his dick deep into her cunt.

Nick was repositioning himself, rising up above me, then coming down, his tattooed body hugging me close, his thighs moving between mine as his prick sought for the entrance to my twat. A moment later he was inside, thrusting strongly, guiding me back towards the peak. Polly and I were stretched out side by side, as Alex and Nick fucked us both. The water bed rippled beneath us.

Polly turned her head towards me, and I twisted mine in her direction. We had just begun to kiss when I achieved my first climax. I moaned rapturously, my hands clutching at Nick's back. But I was unable to keep him in me, and he started to pull away. I freed my lips from Polly's mouth, noticing that Alex was also withdrawing from her cunt.

He and Nick changed places. Within seconds Nick was inside Polly, screwing her furiously. Alex kneeled between my thighs, his hands unfastening my bra and pushing it aside, then reaching for my panties. I raised my hips, allowing him to drag the garment off me, and I was left with only my black stockings and suspender belt. And then it was my turn to be fucked by Alex. His thick moustache tickled my lips as his face came down to kiss mine, and he pumped strongly into me. Polly was next to me, being shafted by Nick, his cock still warm and wet from my cunt.

Throughout this, the other three had kept talking, saying how terrific it all was and that it was the best fucking they'd ever had. But I'd been unable to do anything apart from gasp in pleasure ever since they'd thrown me down onto the bed.

Now Alex spoke again, but it was a different kind of voice he used, more casual, not panting with lust. "I can't hold it much longer," he said.

"Alright," said Murphy. "Nick, what about you? Can we make it simultaneous?"

"No," Nick replied. "I've got a while yet."

"Fine," Murphy told him. "Pull out, Alex, give her it between the tits."

I gripped Alex's buttocks, trying to hold him inside me. All I wanted was a few more strokes to give me a second orgasm. But he pulled free, moving his legs so that he kneeled astride me, his hips above my waist. He leaned down over me, holding his cock out, touching it to the flesh between my breasts. I put my hands on my boobs, pressing them together, catching Alex's prick between them as he began to rub it to and fro. I watched as his glans retreated into the softness of my breasts, before jerking itself towards my chin again.

Then Alex became still, his hips pushed forward, his dick stretching between my breasts – and it started to spurt, gushing a series of hot creamy jets onto my neck and throat.

I raised my head. The spunk trickled down across my breasts, rolling off my flesh and dripping to the bed. I reached out and took hold of Alex's cock, just below where it was sticky from the last drops of oozing spunk, and I wiped it dry with my hair. He allowed me to do it, although then he started to move away. I didn't want that. Because of my unfulfilled desire, I still needed his prick inside me. It was already losing some of its rigidity, but it would have been fat enough for me to rub against my clit.

"No," I begged, speaking for the first time since I'd been brought into the room.

"Tell him what you want," Murphy ordered, asking me to improvise some dialogue.

"Fuck me again," I said to Alex. "Fuck me again. Fuck me again!"

Alex glanced at Nick, who was still screwing his way into Polly, then he looked at me again. He sat down on the edge of the bed, and leaned back. He held his knob in one hand, pointing it upwards.

"Climb on," he told me. "I'll give you the ride of your life."

I did as I was told, straddling him, my toes touching the floor, lowering my twat onto his cock, feeling it bury itself to the hilt. I sighed with contentment as his hips began to rock, pushing his tool against my vaginal walls. As he rubbed up and down, I clenched my cunt, pushing myself against him.

"Soon, Murphy," said Nick, from next to me. "Where do you want it?"

"You both gave it to Polly yesterday," Murphy told him, but he was looking at me. "So give it to her today, all over her face."

Nick pulled his prick free from Polly's gaping twat. He slid across, grasping his cock and holding the glans a few inches from my face. Alex was still fucking me, and I could feel the build up of tension within my twat which promised imminent orgasm. Nick's hand slid back and forth on his shaft, aiming it towards me, masturbating for the final strokes.

We climaxed together, my internal explosion coinciding with Nick's eruption of semen. I opened my mouth in a silent cry of victory, and at the same time the first throw of spunk hit the side of my face. I turned my head, my hand reaching for Nick's cock, guiding it between my lips and sucking him dry in my fever of passion.

Polly slid her head between Nick's crotch and my face, licking the length of his prick between his balls and my mouth, her tongue sliding onto my cheek and lapping at the splash of spunk. Nick withdrew his knob from between my lips, and Polly opened her mouth to take him in. But before she could, I pushed Nick aside and thrust out my tongue, showing her the spunk which lay in a thick film across it. Her tongue licked greedily at mine, sucking off the creamy liquid and swallowing it down.

Alex had seen Polly's eagerness for Nick's tool, and he withdrew his shaft from my cunt and offered it to her. Nick's cock was few inches from her mouth also, and she took one prick in each of her hands, drawing them both towards her lips and sucking in each engorged tip.

All there was left for me was Polly's cunt. So I made it mine, burying my head between her legs and shoving my tongue against her clitoris. Soon after, I felt a hand on my own twat. I didn't know whose it was, and neither did I care. All that mattered was the way the expert fingers stroked my clit and rubbed against my labia, bringing me off for the third sensationally ecstatic time.

Finally we all lay exhausted out on the bed, our limbs tangled, bodies intertwined, fingers and tongues still clutching or licking at the nearest cock or cunt. If this was what making movies was all about, I decided, then it was the life for me.

"Okay, gang," I heard Murphy say. "That's it."

The crew started to put away their equipment. Polly, Nick and Alex climbed from the water bed and left the room. But I continued to lie where I was, flat on my back, legs wide apart, my arms thrown out by my sides.

"You okay?" Murphy asked.

I nodded lethargically.

"You did fine," he told me. Then he smiled. "Not bad for a beginner."

But I still didn't move.

"Is there anything you want?"

"Another orgasm would be nice," I told him.

Murphy laughed. "You'll go far," he predicted.

He was right. That was my first porn movie, but it was by no means the last. Over the next few years, I fucked and sucked more than anyone else in the business. But it wasn't just a matter of quantity, it was also the quality of my sexual performances which took me to the top of my chosen profession. I enjoyed every moment, each drop of spunk, all my myriad orgasms.

If I had the chance, there's only one thing I'd change: I'd want more of it!

ELEVEN

It seemed strange going back to my home town after so long away. Nothing had changed, although the place appeared to have grown smaller. It was difficult to realise that I'd spent most of my life here, although it had hardly been living – not compared with what I'd done since.

I'd come back because of Carole. Out of nowhere, an invitation had arrived to her wedding. At first I was tempted to ignore it, simply to send her a large vibrator as a wedding present and let her make up her own mind about its implications. But after so long, I was no longer angry at Carole's desertion – she'd discovered the pleasures of the penis earlier than me, that was all. I envied her for that. It would be good to see her again and to meet her future husband, a guy called Vince.

I arrived in town the day before the wedding. In the evening I went off for a meal and a few drinks with the bride and groom and half a dozen of their friends, including a petite dark haired girl called Joan who was to be the bridesmaid. It was traditional for a couple to spend their last free evening apart, with friends of their own sex, but it was clear that Carole and Vince didn't want any such separation.

After Carole had introduced me to Vince and we shook hands, he kept watching me. "I'm sure I've seen you before," he said.

"It's not a very big town," I told him. "You probably saw me around when I lived here."

I didn't remember Vince, but that didn't mean much.

When I'd lived there, I didn't have any interest in men. Vince was heavily built, he reminded me of a wrestler, but his face was round and childlike and didn't seem to match his body.

Carole and I didn't have much chance to talk to one another that evening, although the few words which we did exchange reminded me how much we'd once had in common – and not just as sex partners. She insisted that I spend the night with her. Up until then, she and Vince usually alternated their nights at each other's flat, but Carole didn't think it was proper that they should do so immediately before the wedding. Not that Vince would have been able to do much: he got so drunk that he had to be carried out at closing time and driven home by his best man.

Both Carole and I knew that her invitation to me was purely platonic. We would go to bed in the same room, but all we'd do was talk as we used to – before the first time that we'd made love. Whatever we'd done was in the past, something we could both fondly remember. But there was no way we could return. We were different people now.

Even when Carole stripped off and stood naked in front of me, I merely watched her nude body with admiration, not lust. She was as attractive as ever, perhaps even better looking than a few years ago, her figure more developed. She'd been a girl when I'd known her, but now she was a grown woman. No longer with girlish ringlets, her raven hair was styled in the latest fashion.

Carole worked at the local hospital, as an administrative secretary. She didn't know what I did, and I hadn't said. Not because I was ashamed of making blue movies, but because she never asked me. Had she done, I'd probably have told her the truth simply to observe her reaction.

"It's so nice to see you again," Carole said. "This is just like old times."

"Not quite," I pointed out.

"Not quite," she agreed, grinning. "Do you want the bathroom first, or shall I?"

"You take it first," I said, beginning to strip off my own clothes. "Unless you want to share it – for old times' sake." I knew she'd refuse, and she was aware that I was only kidding.

Carole nodded, yawning. We were both tired, exhausted by the late hour and the quantity of alcohol we'd consumed. While she went into the bathroom, I lay on the spare bed. I must have drowsed, because when I next looked up Carole was standing by my side, staring down at my nude body.

"Do you think I should get married?" she asked.

"It's a bit late to ask that now," I told her. "Vince seems a great guy." I was exaggerating, because I hardly knew a thing about Carole's future husband.

She was still studying me, her eyes taking in my breasts, my cunt.

"Whatever a girl can do for you," I told her, "a man can do better. You've got a cunt of your own, so you don't need another. But a cock, that's a different matter."

"I know. That's what I'm thinking about. If I marry Vince, then I'll be stuck with just his prick."

I wondered if she was joking, but her expression was totally serious.

"You only need one," I assured her, although from my own vast experience I knew that wasn't necessarily the case. I've made films where I've taken on two or three, even four or five cocks at the same time; I've been in others where the final scene was several knobs all gushing over my nude body at once. But that's showbiz. For most practical purposes, one dick is sufficient. "And you know that Vince's tool is in good working order, I presume?"

"I suppose so," Carole muttered, and she walked over to her own bed, climbing naked between the sheets. "Oh fuck! She sat up suddenly.

"What's the problem?" I asked, also sitting up.

"It's Vince's suit," she told me. "I collected it from the tailor's today, and he was meant to pick it up."

"It can be done tomorrow," I told her, as I stood and reached for my towel.

"No it can't. It's unlucky for the bride and groom to see each other before the wedding."

"Then I'll take the suit to Vince in the morning. You're not getting married till two o'clock, so there's plenty of time."

"Would you?" asked Carole. "Would you go around with it?"

"Of course I will."

"That's good," she said, sighing and lying down again.

I went into the bathroom. By the time I returned, Carole was fast asleep.

In the morning Joan came around to supervise Carole's next few hours, which would start with taking her to the hairdresser and conclude by making sure that she arrived at the church on time. After breakfast, I went to deliver Vince's suit to him.

After ringing the doorbell to his flat a number of times and waiting about five minutes, I was beginning to think that either Vince hadn't made it home last night or else I was at the wrong address. But finally the door opened a few inches, and Vince's face appeared. It no longer looked quite so childlike. His eyes were bloodshot, his cheeks and chin covered in dark stubble, his brown hair tangled. It was obvious he'd only just woken up. He stared at me without a trace of recognition.

"I've brought your suit, Vince," I told him, holding up the plastic bag as evidence.

He frowned, then slowly nodded in realisation. "Oh, yeah," he muttered. "Thanks." The door swung further open, and Vince disappeared into the depths of his flat.

I went inside, closed the door and followed him into the small kitchen. It was dark, and I pulled the cord to open the venetian blind. Vince groaned, blinking against the sudden light, holding up his hands to his face. He was leaning back against the sink unit. I noticed his pyjama jacket was on inside out, while the pants were slung low on his hips, his pubic hairs curling over the elastic waistband.

"Want a cup of coffee?" he asked, letting his hands drop from his eyes. Then he hitched up his pyjamas to a more decent level.

"Sit down," I told him, because he looked as though he'd fall down if he didn't. I put his suit on the back of a chair. "I'll make the coffee. Would you like something to eat?"

"Don't mention food," he said, one hand holding his stomach and the other going to his mouth as though to prevent himself being sick. He sat down at the table. "Just coffee, thanks. You'll have to excuse me, I don't usually get in this state."

"That's okay," I said. I found a jar of instant coffee, then started filling the kettle. "It isn't every day you get married."

Vince leaned his elbows on the table, resting his head in the palms of his hands. "I feel awful," he said, which I'd already deduced. "I don't think I can make it there. Two o'clock. What time is it now?"

"It's ten," I told him. "There's plenty of time. You haven't got to do anything much, have you?"

"Recover. My head feels as though it's been kicked by an elephant."

"Have you got any aspirin?"

"Somewhere. On the table next to the bed, I think."

"I'll go and have a look."

It was only a small flat, three rooms including the kitchen and bathroom, but the last room was of a fair size and served as both bedroom and living room. I went through into there, drawing back the curtains and opening the window to take away the smell of sweat and tobacco and stale beer. The room was a dump, scattered with dirty dishes and empty bottles, discarded clothes and old newspapers, while uncased CDs lay everywhere. The stereo was still lit up, and I located the button to switch it off. There was a television in the corner, a video recorder on the shelf below. The bed was against the far wall, its covers spilling onto the ground. I found the aspirin bottle and took it back into the kitchen, gave Vince two tablets and a glass of water, then I poured the boiling water from the kettle into two coffee cups.

"You're right," said Vince, referring to what I'd said earlier. "I don't have much to do. Shave, have a bath, wash my hair. Then I'll be as good as new." He raised the cup to his lips, took a sip, and added, "I hope."

"Of course you will," I said.

"How was Carole this morning?" he asked.

"She was fine. She sent her love."

"I wonder about Mac," he said, almost to himself.

"Who's he?"

"My best man."

As Mac had driven Vince here yesterday night, he must have been more sober than the groom – in fact everyone had been much more sober than Vince.

"I'd better phone him," Vince continued. "He was going to come around here later. I ought to make sure he got home okay. All I can remember is getting into his car last night. I've no idea how I got to bed." He rose unsteadily to his feet, then sat down again.

"I'll phone him for you," I said. "Don't worry about him. All you've got to think about is making yourself presentable."

"I suppose so," Vince agreed.

"If you want, I'll stay here until he arrives. I'll make sure you don't fall asleep in the bath."

"Would you? That's great. I don't particularly want to be by myself. It'll be nice just to know you're here."

"You give me Mac's number, and I'll phone him while you're in the bathroom."

"Right. Make yourself at home. Put the stereo on if you like."

Vince locked himself away to get cleaned up. I phoned Mac, who said he'd be around in a couple of hours and take the groom for a couple of drinks; I passed on the first part of the message, but not the second. Then I went through into the main room, thinking of Vince's remark about making myself at home. I didn't know how he was able to live in such messy surroundings. I picked my way through the junk and looked through his scattered collection of music. There was nothing that appealed to me and I switched on the television instead.

The set came on, but there was no picture. I tried the channel buttons on the remote, but nothing happened. Then

I realised it was the video control, and I pressed the play button. The television screen flickered, then settled down to show a close-up of a blonde girl fellating a sturdy cock.

The girl was me!

I watched in amazement. I'd very rarely seen my films; I simply wasn't that interested. Once the movie was in the can and I'd been paid, that was it as far as I was concerned. But now I was fascinated to watch myself in action. I sat on the floor, leaning back against a chair to gaze at the screen.

I tried to remember the film and when it had been made, but I didn't have much information to go on yet. Just me and a prick in my mouth, but that included almost every movie I'd been in. The cock itself provided no clue, because although they varied a lot this one seemed typical of those I'd sucked throughout my career. My tongue stroked the swollen purple glans, my lips rubbing against the shaft as I drew it deeper into my mouth then let it slide almost out again.

How many people were in the film? Was it just me and one guy, or what? All I could do was sit and wait.

After a couple of minutes, my video image pulled the throbbing wet cock from my lips. The camera followed it down as I aimed its tip at my right breast, and it began to spurt its seed onto my flesh. The camera zoomed in, focusing on the come as it dripped down my boob and hung from my nipple. The frame froze for ten seconds, and then the screen blanked.

I still couldn't recall which film it was, but that was hardly surprising considering the countless porn epics in which I'd featured. I pressed the rewind button. The cassette wound back towards the beginning of the tape and switched off automatically. Pushing down the play button, I watched the movie from the beginning.

As soon as it started and I saw the car, I remembered. It

was one of the first films I'd made for Mark, a twenty minute short in which I appeared with another girl and a guy.

I couldn't recall the man's name, but the girl was Lena, who I'd originally met when I'd made my one softcore video for Colin. Her big breasts made her very popular, and we'd been in a number of porn films together.

In this movie we were driving along in an open-topped sports car, Lena behind the wheel. It was a summer day, and the wind blew through our hair. We wore very little because of the heat: sleeveless T-shirts, our nipples clearly visible as they pressed hard against the thin material; brief skirts which came as high as our crotches. The camera studied our bare legs and braless breasts. We were laughing and chatting as we sped along the narrow country road, and my hand rested lightly on Lena's thigh.

As we turned a corner, suddenly there was a man on a bicycle coming towards us. Lena spun the wheel frantically, but the bike went flying into the air. The car had hit it – or so it appeared on screen. The car braked, and we both jumped out, running towards the fallen man. He was lying on his back on the grass verge, unconscious. He wore a pair of lycra shorts and a racing shirt with the number 69 printed across it. His cycle helmet was still fastened on his head, secured by the strap under the chin.

Lena and I knelt over him anxiously, feeling for his pulse, relieved when we found it. We stared down the road, looking for assistance, but there was no one in sight. We quickly debated what we should do, whether we ought to carry him to the car and drive him to the nearest hospital; but we decided to give him the kiss of life in the hope that would revive him. Lena took off the cyclist's helmet and bent down, tugging his jaw so that his mouth opened, then putting her lips to his. I knelt across his chest, pushing up his shirt to reveal a forest of dark curls, and I pressed my hands down across his ribs, as if attempting to force his lungs into action.

After a minute or so, we realised that we'd succeeded. He was breathing properly, and we smiled in satisfaction to one another. But neither of us moved. We glanced at each other, then down at the man beneath us – and our smiles broadened into grins. Lena resumed kissing the man, her tongue licking at his unmoving lips and exploring his mouth. I climbed off him and moved around to his hips, tugging at his tight shorts and yanking them down to expose his half erect cock. I took it in both of my hands, stroking it up and down until it become fully rigid. Then it was the turn of my mouth: I leaned over his groin, my tongue darting out to meet the end of his prick, licking all around the ridge beneath the glans, and finally drawing as much of his shaft between my lips as I could.

Lena was watching. She realised that I had the best of the deal, and she came over to me, pushing her face next to mine, licking at the rider's testicles and the base of his tool. We kissed his cock on either side – until Lena shouldered me away and claimed the penis for herself. I backed off and stood up, looking annoyed, hands on hips as I watched Lena tasting her prize. Then I looked at the man's face, and I grinned as an idea came to me. Swiftly, without raising my skirt, I pulled off my panties and squatted down over his face. My skirt fell across his head as I slid my hips backwards and forwards.

Letting go of the saliva-coated prick, Lena followed my example. She dropped her own briefs, but also removed her skirt to display her brown pubic curls. Then she lowered herself onto the man's cock, holding it upright as she slowly descended. The shaft vanished into her twat. We were facing one another, rubbing ourselves against the supine male beneath us. I stripped off my T-shirt and unzipped the side of my skirt, letting the garment drop to the grass. The camera moved in to show the guy's nose rubbing against the pink flesh of my clitoris.

Lena also peeled off her T-shirt, and we bent towards each other. Our hands caressed each other's tits. Our mouths moved close, tongues inching out to touch one another's. The camera zoomed in for a series of closeups – of our lips against each other's, of the cock sliding in and out of Lena's juicy labia, of my blonde cunt curls tickling the cyclist's face. Which was when his eyes blinked open. He didn't move for a few seconds, but then his arms slid up my body to cup my breasts.

When he'd returned to full awareness, he began to take a more positive role in what was happening. He rolled Lena on her back and proceeded to fuck her; his head was turned up so that his tongue could probe into my twat, while I crouched over him.

Watching myself on the screen, I began to feel my desire rising and my labia became moist. I pulled my dress up to my crotch, rubbing my pubis, then slipping two fingers inside the edge of my panties and stroking my clitoris.

On the television, I took Lena's place and the man began to screw me instead of her, while my tongue licked at Lena's cunt as she knelt above me. Our positions changed again, and we lay in a triangular formation on the grass. Now it was the turn of Lena's tongue to flicker in and out of my pulsing twat, while the man's mouth was locked against her cunt, his cock between my lips.

This was almost where I'd started watching the film, but

my eyes didn't stray from the screen as I brought the cyclist to his climax again, his spunk jetting against my breast. My breath was coming faster and faster as I finger-fucked myself. And when the screen blanked, I realised that I wasn't alone.

I turned my head, and Vince was standing there. His hair was wet, he was clean-shaven – and he was naked, his stubby cock erect.

"I knew I'd seen you before," he said. "I didn't know you were a celebrity." He licked at his lips. "You told me earlier that Carole sent her love. So how about you giving me it?"

I stood up. This had happened before. When men found out that I made porn movies, they assumed I was an easy fuck. All they had to do was flash their tool – exactly as Vince was doing. But right at that moment, his stiff penis was exactly what I needed.

I didn't speak; I simply pulled off my clothes and beckoned to him. Then I turned around, winding back the video two-thirds of the way to the beginning and switching it on play. I lay on the floor in front of the television, lying so that I could watch the screen where I was tugging down the stricken rider's shorts and extracting his cock. It was longer and fatter than Vince's.

Vince knelt down between my legs, staring at me and muttering. He was saying how beautiful and gorgeous I was, but I hardly listened. His hands stroked my contours, rubbing at my breasts, fingering the hairs which fringed my cunt. He leaned towards me, offering his knob to my mouth. But that wasn't where I wanted it. I reached for his prick with my hand, squeezing and stroking it, pushing it down towards my twat.

He got the message and shoved his cock into me. I sighed as his hot flesh slid between my wet cunt lips. He began to fuck me. I lay almost still, letting him do it all, while over his shoulder I watched the video of my past exploits. Vince kept thrusting himself deep into me, his hips swaying slightly from side to side for extra friction, grunting with every jerk of his pelvis.

It didn't take long for him to come, but luckily I was almost ready. As his spunk shot deep into my cunt, it spurred my own orgasm, and I opened my mouth and moaned ecstatically. Vince collapsed on top of me, panting heavily. I began to rock my hips up and down, rubbing my clit against the base of his shaft, bringing myself off within a minute. By that time, my video image again had a few inches of firm cock in her mouth.

But I didn't need that now. Vince had fulfilled my requirements. He withdrew, totally spent and limp. I watched for the third time the video prick squirting its gushing come onto my breast. Then I reached across and switched off the machine.

Vince looked at me uncertainly from the corner of his eye, half-smirking, half-ashamed. "Er . . . ," he mumbled. "You won't tell Carole . . ."

"Tell her what?" I asked as I stood up, feeling a drop of spunk roll down the inside of my thigh. I picked up my clothes, walked past Vince and went through into the bathroom, locking it behind me. After a few seconds I heard the door handle turn. I ignored it and stepped into the shower, pulling down the shower head and switching on a warm spray, aiming it up into my cunt and rinsing out Vince's semen.

When I was dry, I dressed and left the room. Vince was

watching another replay of the video, sitting naked in the chair by the television. He stood up as I entered, his almost vertical knob held optimistically in his hand.

I shook my head, smiling slightly. "It's your wedding day, remember?" I said. "You'd better save that for your honeymoon – and for Carole."

Vince shrugged, then scratched his chin. "Did you, er, like that? Was it, uh, any good?"

"It was just perfect," I assured him, and at the time it had been. "How about you?"

He nodded, grinning, and a moment later the doorbell rang. Vince glanced anxiously at me.

"Back into the bathroom," I suggested. "I'll answer it."

Vince headed for the bathroom. I switched off the video, then went to the door at the end of the hall and opened it.

"Hello," said Mac, staring at me in surprise.

"Hello," I said. I gestured for him to enter. "I came to bring Vince's suit. He's in the bathroom. I'd better be going now. See you both later."

"Yeah," said Mac, gazing at me. "I'll see you."

He hadn't recognised me yesterday, but maybe since then he'd watched Vince's video – although in porn movies who looks at the girls' faces?

The wedding was two hours later, and an hour after that the reception began in a hired room in the town's best hotel. There was plenty to eat, and far more to drink, and I made sure that I ate and drank my fill. Vince and I ignored one another, but Mac cornered me for several minutes, obviously fancying his chances. I was certain Vince hadn't said anything to his best man about what had occurred that morning.

I also realised Mac hadn't watched the video, otherwise his approach to me would have been very different.

Carole looked stunning in her full length virginal white silk wedding dress, trimmed with lace. She was still wearing it during the reception, although she removed the veil. After the formal meal, the tables were cleared for dancing. I managed to avoid Mac's invitation as a partner by saying that I'd eaten too much and didn't want to vomit all over him. He didn't speak to me again after that.

Joan, the bridesmaid, had a similar problem – except that she'd drunk too much champagne and really was sick. Carole had booked a hotel room where she could change out of her wedding dress before leaving with Vince for their honeymoon, and so she asked me to go up with her and help her out of the elaborate garment.

"We haven't had much chance to talk properly, have we?" she added. "I fell asleep last night, and this morning you took Vince's suit. Thanks for that, by the way."

"No trouble," I told her. We left the room where everyone was laughing and talking and drinking and dancing. It was only then that I realised I was far from sober. But it was a positive feeling, happy and relaxed. We took the lift to the third floor and walked along the corridor to one of the rooms, going inside and closing the door behind us.

"You look really great, you know," I said, gazing at Carole in admiration.

"That's exactly the way I feel, too," she replied, spinning around so that the skirt of her dress swirled up above her knees. "Great. Absolutely great."

I continued staring at her, remembering my wedding present to Vince that morning, and thinking that to be fair Carole ought to receive a similar gift. Last night, although I'd seen her naked, I'd experienced no passionate desire for her body. But it was different now, and I wasn't certain why. I'd drunk plenty the previous night, too, so that couldn't be it. Perhaps it was because of Vince, that despite my two orgasms I hadn't been properly fulfilled. Or maybe it was because Carole was now wed. Legally, she belonged to another – and I ached to take her first, before Vince could consummate their marriage.

"Can you undo these buttons here?" Carole asked, turning her back on me.

I didn't move, and after a moment Carole spun around and looked directly at me. She'd been smiling before, but now her expression was serious.

"What's wrong?" she asked.

I shook my head, forcing a bright smile. "Nothing," I said. "I was just looking at you, remembering . . ."

"You looked sad."

"I'm not," I assured her. "Not at all." I grinned. "I felt jealous of all those guys before, kissing the bride."

"You shouldn't have been," Carole said. She came towards me, holding her arms wide, pulling me against her. We embraced, and I felt the softness of her breasts against my own boobs. I noticed a tear in the corner of her right eye, and it trickled slowly down her cheek. I put my lips to her face, licking it away. Carole turned her head, and our lips gently met. Tentatively, I kissed the bride.

It was Carole's mouth which parted first, her tongue creeping out and pushing its way between my lips. My own tongue accepted the challenge, thrusting against the intruder, then admitting defeat and surrendering, caressing the invading tongue as it explored my mouth.

I was back where I'd started, so long ago.

But as I lifted Carole's wedding dress and discovered that she wore no panties, and I stroked her damp curls then slid my fingers into her eager cunt, I knew this was another beginning.